Ex-Spinster by Christmas
(House of Haverstock Series, Book 4)

Ever pragmatic, Lady Caroline Ponsby has given up
hope she'll ever receive a proposal of marriage from
Christopher Perry, the wealthy man she's adored for
almost two years. She is determined to be an ex-
spinster by Christmas. To that end, she has invited a
prospective suitor to spend Christmas with her
family. She knows very well that Lord Brockton
would love to get his hands on her dowry, and she'd
love to be a married woman with a home and family
of her own.

The very idea of his Lady Caroline throwing herself
away on the likes of the vile Lord Brockton rankles
Christopher Perry. A pity he cannot offer for her
himself, but a duke's daughter is too far above his
touch, given his family's humble origins.
Nevertheless, Christopher attends the Duke of
Aldridge's Christmas house party with the intention
of thwarting Lady Caroline's grave misalliance with
Brockton. If only he's not too late . . .

Some of the praise for Cheryl Bolen's writing:

"One of the best authors in the Regency romance field today." – *Huntress Reviews*

"Bolen's writing has a certain elegance that lends itself to the era and creates the perfect atmosphere for her enchanting romances." – *RT Book Reviews*

The Counterfeit Countess (Brazen Brides, Book 1)
Daphne du Maurier award finalist for Best Historical Mystery

"This story is full of romance and suspense. . . No one can resist a novel written by Cheryl Bolen. Her writing talents charm all readers. Highly recommended reading! 5 stars!" – *Huntress Reviews*

"Bolen pens a sparkling tale, and readers will adore her feisty heroine, the arrogant, honorable Warwick and a wonderful cast of supporting characters." – *RT Book Reviews*

One Golden Ring (Brazen Brides, Book 2)
"*One Golden Ring*...has got to be the most PERFECT Regency Romance I've read this year." – *Huntress Reviews*

Holt Medallion winner for Best Historical, 2006

Lady By Chance (House of Haverstock, Book 1)
Cheryl Bolen has done it again with another sparkling Regency romance. . .Highly recommended – *Happily Ever After*

The Bride Wore Blue (Brides of Bath, Book 1)
Cheryl Bolen returns to the Regency England she knows so well. . .If you love a steamy Regency with a fast pace, be sure to pick up *The Bride Wore Blue*. – *Happily Ever After*

With His Ring (Brides of Bath, Book 2)
"Cheryl Bolen does it again! There is laughter, and the interaction of the characters pulls you right into the book. I look forward to the next in this series." – *RT Book Reviews*

The Bride's Secret (Brides of Bath, Book 3)
*(*originally titled *A Fallen Woman)*
"*W*hat we all want from a love story...Don't miss it!"
– *In Print*

To Take This Lord (Brides of Bath, Book 4)
*(*originally titled *An Improper Proposal)*
"Bolen does a wonderful job building simmering sexual tension between her opinionated, outspoken heroine and deliciously tortured, conflicted hero." – *Booklist of the American Library Association*

My Lord Wicked
Winner, International Digital Award for Best Historical Novel of 2011.

With His Lady's Assistance (Regent Mysteries, Book 1)
"A delightful Regency romance with a clever and personable heroine matched with a humble, but intelligent hero. The mystery is nicely done, the romance is enchanting and the secondary characters are enjoyable." – *RT Book Reviews*

Finalist for International Digital Award for Best Historical Novel of 2011.

A Duke Deceived
"A Duke Deceived is a gem. If you're a Georgette Heyer fan, if you enjoy the Regency period, if you like a genuinely sensuous love story, pick up this first novel by Cheryl Bolen." – *Happily Ever After*

Books by Cheryl Bolen

Regency Romance

House of Haverstock Series
Lady by Chance (Book 1)
Duchess by Mistake (Book2)
Countess by Coincidence (Book 3)
Ex-Spinster by Christmas (Book 4)

Brazen Brides Series
Counterfeit Countess (Book 1)
His Golden Ring (Book 2)
Oh What A (Wedding) Night (Book 3)
Marriage of Inconvenience (Book 4)

The Brides of Bath Series:
The Bride Wore Blue (Book 1)
With His Ring (Book 2)
The Bride's Secret (Book 3)
To Take This Lord (Book 4)
Love in the Library (Book 5)
A Christmas in Bath (Book 6)

The Regent Mysteries Series:
With His Lady's Assistance (Book 1)
A Most Discreet Inquiry (Book 2)
The Theft Before Christmas (Book 3)
An Egyptian Affair (Book 4)

The Earl's Bargain
My Lord Wicked
His Lordship's Vow
A Duke Deceived

Novellas:
Christmas Brides (3 Regency Novellas)
Only You

Inspirational Regency Romance
Marriage of Inconvenience

Romantic Suspense
Texas Heroines in Peril Series:
    Protecting Britannia
    Capitol Offense
    A Cry in the Night
    Murder at Veranda House

Falling for Frederick

American Historical Romance
A Summer to Remember (3 American Historical Romances)

World War II Romance
It Had to be You

Ex-Spinster

By Christmas

(House of Haverstock Series, Book 4)

Cheryl Bolen

House of Haverstock

Charles Upton —————— Lydia Upton —————— Elizabeth Upton ——— Other Siblings
(Marquees of
Haverstock)
          Ralph "Morgie"
          Morgan

Anna de
Mouchet

                   Kate Upton
                   James Upton
                   Mary Upton
                   Charlotte Upton

Philip Ponsby —————— Margaret Ponsby — Caroline Ponsby — Other Siblings
(Duke of
Aldridge)
        John Beauclerc
        (Earl of
        Finchley)

            Christopher
            Perry

                   John Ponsby
                   Compton Ponsby
                   Harold Ponsby
                   Sarah Ponsby
                   Clair Ponsby

                   (Rothcomb-
                   Smedley)

$\mathcal{C}$hapter 1

"Have you taken leave of your senses?" Margaret's eyes widened and her mouth gaped open. "How could you possibly consider marrying Lord Brockton when you're in love with Christopher Perry?"

Lady Caroline Ponsby sighed. "Over the course of a year and a half Mr. Perry has yet to proclaim his affections for me."

"But he loves you. We all know it."

"I thought Mr. Perry loved me," Caro said with a sigh. "But I was mistaken."

"You are *not* mistaken! He rarely goes a day without seeing you. He's no longer interested in any woman except you."

"But being wed is as disagreeable to Mr. Perry as the pox. I'm tired of being the pitiable spinster. It's been four years since I came out, and I have failed most deplorably to attract a husband."

"You most decidedly have *not* failed most deplorably! Have not eleven men sought your hand in marriage?"

Caro's gaze narrowed. "That was *before* Christopher Perry."

"Before you fell in love with him at first

sight. Trust those initial instincts." Propped up on a mound of frilly pillows, Margaret sipped at her chocolate. "I shouldn't be telling you about so indelicate a subject—you being a maiden. But John—who never speaks of things like feelings—said he believes you're the reason Mr. Perry dismissed his mistress." Margaret's lashes lowered and a smile curled her lips. "Dear John said a man in love could not wish to lie with a woman other than the one who's engaged his affections."

Caro had a very good idea why her sister smiled. She was thinking of lying with that husband over whom she was so besotted. She eyed the sister who looked so much like her. Even the colour of their flaxen hair was identical—as was the blue of their eyes. Still swaddled in fine white linen sheets and framed by the opulence of the turquoise bed curtains of rich silk, Margaret was finishing up the last of her morning chocolate.

Margaret had the good fortune to have most happily wed the man of her dreams, and a year and a half later she still continued to glow like a newlywed bride.

Caro's chest tightened. *I will never experience such bliss*. She diverted her comments. "I flirted with Lord Brockton at the Hawkleys' ball last week, and he was most receptive."

Margaret rolled her eyes. "Then I daresay he'll be number twelve."

"If he does offer, I'll accept him. I want a home of my own." Her voice softened. "I want to have children. Do you know how painful it is to be with my family and to know I'm the only one without a child?"

"I know how much you love children. You will have them. But, pray, don't wed a man you cannot love in order to become a mother. Do you want to be trapped in a marriage like Lady Kate and her unfortunate husband?"

"I would never bring such shame upon our brother as she's brought to Lord Haverstock with her incessant affairs."

"Speaking of our brother, I shall beg him to *not* permit you to wed Brockton—if Lord Brockton should ask."

Caro shook her head most emphatically. "I beg that you do not. I've wasted nearly two years on a man who's never going to come up to scratch. Lord Brockton is a good enough catch, and he's certainly as handsome as Mr. Perry."

"One does not marry a man simply because he's handsome. You know as well as I that Lord Brockton's a libertine. And a fortune hunter."

Caro laughed. "You of all people should know how easily rakes are reformed. Your Lord Finchley—and I will own, Mr. Perry, too—had a raucous reputation." Even when the immature Finchley first married her sister, he had continued with his hedonistic pursuits.

Then he fell in love with Margaret, and love changed him profoundly.

Would Caro ever be able to stop loving Christopher Perry? She had loved him for so long now and so passionately that the very contemplation of severing ties to him was rather like losing a limb.

Even as she stood there in her sister's turquoise bedchamber, Caro's breath grew short when she thought of him. She could almost feel his scorching black eyes peering into hers with a sense of possession. If only she could feel herself in his arms one last time—one last time before she marched out of his life forever.

For weeks now she had endeavored to spend less and less time with Mr. Perry. She had come to need him as an opium eater craves opium. And like an opium addict, she had to withdraw from him in increments.

She wondered if she could ever love Lord Brockton so fiercely. Could she even love him at all?

Margaret's gaze dropped to her crumpled white coverlet as she whispered. "Some rakes *can* be reformed by the love for a wife and child."

Even though she was fully dressed for morning calls in a soft cream-coloured muslin dress, Caro flung herself on the bed beside her sister. "Do you have any idea how fortunate you are?"

"I give thanks every day that I'm married to the only man I have ever loved, that my dear John loves me, that we are blessed with the most perfect child." She peered at the sister who was almost her twin. "Yes, I am well aware of my good fortune."

"La! I shall never be loved as you are. I'm schooling myself to accept that."

Margaret's pitying glance made Caro uncomfortable. She rose from the bed, forced a bright smile, and spoke cheerfully. "Just think. If I can capture Lord Brockton's heart I shall be the envy of every lady in the *ton*!"

"And if you loved him, I'd be most sincerely happy for you. But I know you too well. You cannot make me believe you're *not* still in love with Mr. Perry."

Caro strolled to her sister's writing table and fingered the ink pot, her back to her sister. She had never been able to tell a falsehood without Margaret detecting it. Therefore, she could not face the sister to whom she'd always been closest—not when she was going to tell a lie. She let out a little laugh. "I will own, I once was completely potty over the man, but as time has worn on and I've come to see his flaws, I fancy a change."

"You're lying. I know you love him."

Ignoring her sister, Caro moved to the dressing table and peered at her sister in the looking glass as Margaret came to her feet and moved toward her.

Caro whirled around. "I'm of age. I will marry Lord Brockton with or without my brother's consent. Just as you did with Lord Finchley."

"I pray you'd be half as happy."

Caro took up her muffler and spun it about her neck. "I go back to Aldridge House now to beg that our brother invite Lord Brockton to Glenmont Hall for Christmas.

* * *

She tried to recall if Lord Brockton had ever been to the ducal townhouse in which she'd spent most of her life. She thought not. When she reached her home on Berkeley Square, dear, deaf Barrow admitted her. Aldridge had ordered that the doors be locked at all times after a rash of burglaries in Mayfair in recent weeks.

"Hello, Barrow. Where's my brother?" She allowed him to assist in removing her muffler, frosty cloak, and hat.

The white-haired butler nodded and spoke in his shaky voice. "The duchess has already asked that we cover the furniture in Holland cloths before we leave for Glenmont."

Oh, dear. Barrow must have thought she asked for covers. Did he not know she would never try to usurp the authority of the home's true mistress, her brother's adored wife? Caro must try again. This time she spoke louder. "Aldridge? Where is his grace?"

"His grace is in the library, my lady."

As she moved along the opulent entry corridor beneath a massive, glittering chandelier, she wondered how Lord Brockton's townhome compared to this. All she knew about it was that it was heavily mortgaged and that it was one of the largest houses on Grosvenor Square.

She fancied being mistress of a fine West London home—her own home. She could be the one to order servants to bring out the Holland cloths when they were leaving for the country.

The door to the library was open. Even with a fire blazing, the wood-paneled room was very dark. It took a few seconds before she saw her brother. He sat on a crimson damask sofa in front of the fire, reading, his back to her.

She padded along the Turkey carpet toward him. He looked up, and their gazes locked. "You've been to see our sister, Lady Finchley?" he asked.

Nodding, she came to share the camel-backed sofa. It felt good to sit near the fire. It was beastly cold outside. "We are greatly looking forward to spending the Yule at Glenmont. Speaking of which . . . I beseech you to invite Lord Brockton to join us for the Christmas festivities."

His dark brows shot up. "Brockton?"

She nodded. It had always puzzled her how

three relatively small-boned, fair-complexioned sisters had come from the same womb as her tall, dark-haired brother.

"Whatever for?"

"Because I wish it most profoundly."

His eyes squinted as he peered at her in much the same way he would if she had just turned bright purple. "*You* wish it?"

"Indeed."

"What about that Perry chap? I thought . . . well, I thought there must be an understanding between you two."

She shook her head most vigorously. "Nothing could be further from the truth. He's merely a friend—the best friend of Margaret's husband, so we're thrown together a great deal."

He was silent for a moment. Finally, he nodded. "If you wish, I will invite Lord Brockton, but I beg that you make no rash decisions regarding the fellow until we get to know him better. His reputation is not what I would have hoped for a suitor for my sister."

"You could have said the same about Lord Finchley, and look at what a strong marriage they've forged, how devoted they are to one another."

He chuckled. "If Finchley had asked me for Margaret's hand, I would certainly have forbidden the match."

Caro shrugged. "She *was* of age."

"As are you now." His dark eyes locked

with hers. There was a stern look on his face when he spoke. "Oblige me by taking things slowly."

"You speak as if I have all the time in the world." She stood and stared down at him. "I don't. I'm disgusted with being a spinster." She stalked to the door, then turned back. "I'm grateful that you'll invite his lordship."

* * *

Christopher Perry had come to White's this evening to mingle with his friends one last time before they all scattered to their country houses to celebrate Christmas. As thin as company was there, he began to suspect many had already left London.

At least Finch was there. The two of them sat next to each other at a longer table where several gentlemen were taking a repast beneath a pair of crystal chandeliers blazing with a hundred candles.

Finch sighed. "I do wish you'd come with us to Glenmont for Christmas. If you don't, I'll be forced to spend my time with the two stuffiest fellows in all the kingdom."

Christopher chuckled. "Haverstock and Aldridge?"

Lord Finchley nodded. "Both very fine men and all that, but you know how dull they are."

They might be dull now, Christopher thought, but as younger men they'd cut a merry path. Aldridge even indulged in a long affair with a beautiful Italian countess. Before he married. "Which is one very good reason why I have no intentions of going to Glenmont."

Finch's brows lowered. "And your other reasons?"

"I cannot leave my mother at Christmas."

"Bring her along! Maggie and I are taking my Grandmere. Can't leave her alone, either."

Christopher shook his head as he refilled his glass with wine and passed the bottle to his left. "I said I'd take my mother and the girls to Somersham."

Finch made a face. "What a pity."

"You think your Christmas will be dull!"

His friend gave a mock shudder. "Four females and not another male in sight. I don't envy you."

The three empty chairs across the table were soon filled with Lord Dundee, Lord Brockton, and Robert Cuthbert. They were all around the age of thirty but had a reputation for acting as immature as youths just down from Oxford. There was nothing offensive about Dundee or Cuthbert, but Christopher had never cared for Brockton—and not just because he'd been hovering around Lady Caroline as of late.

He just could not respect the man. Brockton lacked any semblance of honor. An honorable man did not boast about the married women he'd bedded—especially not at the club where the cuckolded husband was a member.

The three men nodded at him and Finch.

As Christopher and Finch directed their attention to their kidney pies, Christopher couldn't help but to overhear the conversation among the three newcomers.

"I daresay, Brockton, you'll be married to a duke's daughter before six weeks have passed," Cuthbert said.

A smile spread on Brockton's face. Christopher attempted to determine what there was about the man that enraptured females so. He supposed he was as fine looking as a woman could hope to attract. Indeed, Christopher had been told that Brockton was considered one of the most handsome men in the kingdom.

He was considerably taller than Christopher and possessed of broad shoulders encased in finely tailored clothing. There was a patrician countenance about his fair face, and his cork-coloured hair was styled in the latest fashion.

Christopher should know. He himself had been called the arbiter of good taste. Of course, Christopher had the fortune to indulge his extravagant eye for finery. Brockton did not. It would surprise Christopher if Brockton's tailor had received a farthing from his aristocratic client in these past two years.

"Indeed," Brockton said. "A duke's daughter with thirty thousand." The man's self-assured cockiness bespoke pride of accomplishment though he'd accomplished nothing by his own merit. Even the goose that laid the golden egg could point to its achievement. All this braggart had to recommend him was a handsome face.

"The duke himself has invited me to spend Christmas with their family," Brockton continued.

Lord Dundee slapped him on his back. "You lucky bugger. And she's beautiful too." He shrugged. "She turned me down the year she came out. I thought at the time she was holding out for a duke."

"I daresay Brockton could be a mere mister like me and still win the lady's hand," Cuthbert said. "Women do seem to flock to him."

"When will you offer for her?" Dundee asked.

Brockton smirked. "Christmas, I think. What better present could a woman seek?"

A more obnoxious man Christopher had never met.

"You're incorrigible," Dundee said with a shake of his head.

Cuthbert sighed. "You're a most fortunate man. I suppose with a lovely wife like that, you'll dismiss Mrs. Johnson."

Brockton's brows lowered. "Being wed will

change nothing—except my pocketbook."

"You don't fancy yourself in love with the lady?" Dundee asked.

Brockton laughed. "I love all women. Never let it be said the Earl of Brockton is in any woman's pocket." He glanced across the table and spoke to Finch. "Say, Finchley, will you and that wife of yours be spending Christmas at Glenmont?"

Finch nodded. "We leave tomorrow."

"As do I. I shall see you there."

Christopher felt as if the contents of his stomach were going to erupt like a spewing volcano. *Dear God, the duke's daughter is my Lady Caroline.*

$\mathcal{C}$hapter 2

He could no longer sit at the same table with that pompous, conceited, insensitive profligate. Half way through the meal, he'd stood and turned to Finch, who looked almost as stricken as Christopher felt. "I'd completely forgotten that I promised to eat with my mother tonight." He nodded at Lord Dundee and Cuthbert, then strode from the chamber.

His coach offered only a slight respite from the biting cold, but his physical condition was the last thing on his mind. A blinding fury bolted through him. How dare that devil try to wed Lady Caroline Ponsby! The man wasn't even worthy of kissing her hand.

And how could a man be such a fool as to seek the bed of his low-born mistress when he had the great honor of marrying that most perfect being? If the damned earl had the good fortune to wed Lady Caroline and if he had the poor sense to be unfaithful to her, Christopher just might have to challenge him to a duel.

It was all Christopher could do to not drive a fist into Lord Brockton's smug face back at White's. Brockton knew Christopher had a prior claim on Lady Caroline. What gentleman would shove himself into another gentleman's territory?

Christopher sighed. Would Brockton have pressed his suit with Lady Caroline if Christopher had been a fellow peer? Was Christopher still not considered a gentleman? Even though his greatest friend was an earl and the woman he had long loved was a duke's daughter, Christopher still didn't feel he belonged to their privileged world.

He laughed a bitter laugh. He could buy everything Lord Brockton and Lord Finchley possessed, and it would barely dent the Perry family fortune, yet Christopher still could not shake the stigma of his Jewish ancestors, dead now for three generations.

Was that why Lady Caroline had been backing away from him? Why she was encouraging Brockton? Or was she moving on because Christopher had failed to ask for her hand?

For more than a year and a half he'd spent time with no other woman. He'd not wanted to be with anyone other than Lady Caroline. He hadn't even desired his mistress. How could he when his hunger for Lady Caroline and only Lady Caroline strummed through him every hour of every day? He'd thought of nothing but making her his own, but he respected and loved her too dearly to lie with her without marriage and respected and loved her too dearly to offer marriage.

The great grandson of a Jewish jeweler was hardly worthy of the daughter of duke.

While he had not lain with her, often he had stolen kisses and gloried in the feel of his adored Lady Caroline in his arms. Even tonight, here in the frigid carriage, the memory of holding her close aroused him.

His breath was ragged when he remembered how compliant she had always been. He smiled when remembering their first scorching kiss and how surprised he had been over her capacity for passion.

Dear God, would she kiss Brockton as she had kissed him?

How could she transfer her affections so easily? For even though Christopher was unworthy of her, he believed Lady Caroline had loved him. Finch had intimated that she expected a proposal of marriage.

But Christopher was too much of a coward. Even after a year and a half, he was still beastly uncomfortable in the presence of her brother, the Duke of Aldridge. The fellow was so serious and lofty. He was sure to look down his aristocratic nose at the Perry family origins.

The Ponsby family dated back to the time of the Conqueror.

He had always pictured Lady Caroline marrying into a family equal to her own in prestige. But never had he thought she'd throw herself away on a scoundrel like Brockton. Could she not see past the man's title and his handsome countenance?

There was not another peer of the realm who could have been a worse choice. She was a very clever girl. Surely Lady Caroline would come to her senses and recognize Brockton's absence of merit.

And if she didn't?

Nothing could be more painful to Christopher. He wanted the best for her. He wanted her to be happy. He loved her.

And despite his own unworthiness, he wanted her for himself. Forever.

But that could never be.

His coach rounded the corner to Piccadilly, and through the fogged-up window Christopher could see the yellow glow of a pair of giant lanterns at either side of the entry to his impressive house. The coachman opened the gates, got back on the box, and drove across the courtyard to the home's front door that was flanked by a pair of smaller lanterns.

Inside, Christopher divested himself of his great coat, hat, and muffler. "Where's my mother?"

"She's in the drawing room listening to your sister at the pianoforte," Whitman said.

Christopher marched up the brightly lit stairway and at the door to the yellow drawing room, he stopped. Augusta was playing the pianoforte, and his enraptured mother was watching her daughter. Mama had every right to be proud of her. Augusta played with exceptional ability. Her talent was something that could not have been purchased with her father's great wealth.

As he watched his mother, Christopher's face softened. She had been a reputed beauty, and at fifty, she was still lovely. So different from him and Augusta, both of whom favored their dark father. Mama's skin was exceedingly pale with rosy cheeks, and her once blonde hair was only partially gray. Her figure bore little sign of spreading as did others of the same age.

Though she missed their father enormously, she never indulged in self pity and never for a moment put her own interests over that of her children and grandchildren.

Augusta looked up at him and smiled, never missing a note.

Following her daughter's gaze, Mama turned to face him. "Ah, Christopher! I never thought to see you home at so early an hour." Her brows lowered as she scrutinized him as a painter studies his subject. "Something's wrong. Whatever is the matter, dearest?"

His mother knew him too well. He shook his head and forced a smile. "Nothing's wrong. I was thinking I'd need a good night's sleep if we're to journey to Somersham tomorrow."

Her tenseness uncoiled. "Come sit by me."

He came to the plump pink silken sofa and kissed his mother's cheek before he sat down. Augusta continued playing, and he found the lovely tune soothing. So was the nearby fire. It was one of those cold nights which made one want to climb upon one's bed, draw shut its velvet curtains, and bury oneself under mounds of blankets.

"I thought Lord Finchley might try to persuade you to spend Christmas with him. Will he and his lovely wife be traveling to the Duke of Aldridge's country home?"

"Yes, and he did invite me." Christopher patted his mother's hand. "And he invited you as well."

"Pshaw! I could never be comfortable around such lofty people. I don't know how you manage. I'd be so humbled in their presence I'd be speechless and cowering."

He chuckled and clasped her hand. "You shouldn't be. You're a far more worthy person than any noblewoman I've ever met. And . . . ," he said with a mischievous gleam in his eye, "none of them dresses with your eye for elegance." Which was true.

His family's fortune might purchase the finest dressmakers and fabrics and jewels, but it could not buy the innate sense of style his mother possessed.

He had inherited it and still did not know if it was a curse or a blessing. It grew tedious being judiciously studied by every young buck who came to town.

"You forget Lady Caroline," she said. "I've met her but once, but I believe you must find her exceedingly worthy."

His gut plunged. He swallowed hard. "She is."

* * *

As Caro stood just off the entry hall of Aldridge House to don her red velvet cloak in preparation for her long drive to Glenmont, she witnessed Lady Haverstock leave the duchess's study and race down the stairs, almost bumping into Caro.

Stunned to see tears streaking Anna Haverstock's beautiful face, she said, "My lady, what's wrong?"

The marchioness merely shook her head and sped to the door. "I'm being a goose."

Caro flew up the stairs and faced the duchess. "What's happened to Lady Haverstock?"

Elizabeth's face was grave. "She's convinced her husband must have a mistress."

"That's the most ridiculous thing I've ever heard! Everyone knows your brother's besotted over her."

"That's what I tried to tell her, but . . . well, she confided something to me that is not fit for a maiden's ears."

"I will never believe Lord Haverstock has a

ladybird. She has validation of that?" Elizabeth shook her blond head. "A ladybird is *not* what I was referring to. It's something else, something about her and her husband."

Caro's brows squeezed together. "Are you saying Lord Haverstock no longer seeks to lie with his wife?"

Her eyes narrow, her hands planted at her hips, the duchess glared at her sister-in-law. "You most certainly are not supposed to know about such."

"Pray, give me credit. I'm many years out of the schoolroom. I know about a man's desires for a woman. I once overheard Lady Haverstock tell you that a man satisfied by his wife would never have reason to seek . . . *release* elsewhere."

Dear merciful heavens, Elizabeth was blushing! Was Caro the only woman in the family who did not get embarrassed by such talk? "I'm not inquiring about your intimacies, dearest."

"Poor Anna. I am so vexed with my brother," Elizabeth said. "He hasn't come to her bed in weeks. She's convinced he doesn't love her anymore." She shrugged. "I know he would never stop loving her. It must be something else."

"He's been very successful in the House in Lords. It can't be that."

"Nor can it be his position at the Foreign Office. Philip would know it if anything was amiss there. I'm so worried about her."

"I'm sure everything will be fine when we all arrive for a relaxing Christmas at Glenmont."

Elizabeth nodded. "Are you sure you don't want to ride with Philip and me?"

"I've already promised Margaret I'd ride with them. In fact, their coach is to collect me soon."

"Philip and I are ready, too."

* * *

"I'm most gratified that you've chosen to ride in our carriage instead of with Elizabeth and Aldridge," Margaret said to Caro, who sat across from her. The rugs spread across their laps and wrapped around their icy feet helped warm them on this frigid afternoon as the Finchley coach rattled along these country roads.

When Caro spotted the bridge at Horsham, she knew they would be at Glenmont within the hour.

"I live with Elizabeth and Aldridge," Caro said, "and therefore welcome the opportunity to spend every minute I can with my almost-twin sister. I thought Grandmere was coming with us?"

"She prefers her own coach. The dowager Lady Haverstock's riding with her since they're such old friends."

Caro eyed Margaret's softly snoring husband, his long legs stretched out across the carriage. He'd slept for the past four hours, ever since they'd left London. She stuck out her lower lip in an exaggerated pout. "I wish we still shared a bedchamber."

Margaret gave her a pitying glance. "Everyone has to grow up, and as much as I miss you, my life is fuller and happier than it's ever been. I wish the same for you in a marital state. With Mr. Perry."

"You've got to get it out of your head that I'm marrying Christopher Perry." Caro's eyes narrowed. "I've moved on and am greatly looking forward to furthering my acquaintance this Christmas with the most handsome lord in the realm."

Margaret's brows lowered, and she spoke in jest. "You speak of my husband?"

To Margaret, there was no finer looking man in the kingdom than her Lord Finchley. "Forgive me. I meant to say the *second* most handsome lord in the kingdom."

" I cannot believe Aldridge has indulged you by asking Lord Brockton to Glenmont. I know he does *not* approve of the man."

"Just because Lord Brockton lost his fortune and needs to marry an heiress does not mean the man is without merit. He's never been anything but a perfect gentleman in my presence."

"I never said he was a *fool*—merely a libertine." Margaret's lids lowered as she looked down at the sleeping babe in her arms.

"I declare," Caro said, eyeing her nephew,

"little Frederick is exactly like his Papa. The movement of the carriage must lull both of them to sleep."

"Indeed. In fact, one night when the nurse was concerned because our little angel wouldn't go to sleep, I rang for the carriage, and Nurse and I rode around Mayfair but for five minutes and Freddie went sound to sleep."

The infant boy did not seem to have inherited any Ponsby characteristics, but that did not detract from Caro's adoration of her nephew. She never tired of looking at him. Or holding him. She felt the same over each of her nephews and her niece. "Even though he's such a babe still, he will be in heaven at Glenmont with all those babies."

"Sadly, Morgie and Lydia's son is no longer a babe. It distresses me that they grow up so fast. At least the Morgans will have a new babe." Margaret eyed her sister. "Did you know they're coming to Glenmont?"

"Yes. Lord Haverstock said he could never celebrate Christmas without Lydia. She's always been his favorite sister."

"When is the new babe expected?" Margaret asked.

"Not until February."

Caro peered from the carriage window. Minutes ago it had been a gray afternoon. Now night was lowering its dark screen over the hilly landscape that would always claim her heart.

She knew all the landmarks around the ancestral home that had been in the Ponsby family for centuries. The far-off spire of the village church signaled that they were just minutes away from Glenmont.

The coachman soon turned onto the long road that cut through Glenmont's vast parkland. A sprinkling of snow covered its winter-bleached grass. They climbed higher until the fourteen chimneys of Glenmont came into view, then its three stories of gray stone. Caro always swelled with pride when she beheld her ancestral home. Glenmont lacked the symmetry of the Palladian mansions that were so much in vogue. The old pile was a hodgepodge of jutting wings and different elevations and windows from every architectural era since the Tudor period. And there wasn't a thing about it she would change.

Lord Finchley began to stir. In the span between breaths, his snoring stopped. His eyelids lifted, and when his gaze met Caro's he snapped into a seated position. "I perceive I've been sleeping."

"I declare," his wife said, "you could sleep amidst the shouting at a cock fight."

He scowled. "My wife is not supposed to know how men act at such an event." He eyed his sleeping son. "Here, allow me to take him. Your arms must be aching."

"My arms never ache from holding Freddie." They exchanged their sleeping son without disturbing his slumber. "And besides, whenever Caro's near, she manages to get rather a good cuddle with him."

Lord Finchley smiled down at his son, then his brows lowered. "Please tell me I did *not* snore in front of Lady Caroline."

"Of course you snored, my dearest," Margaret said.

He eyed Caro from beneath hooded brows. "Terribly sorry. A maiden shouldn't have to be exposed to such."

"But dearest," Margaret said, "Caro professes not to be a maiden much longer. She desires to wed by Christmas."

His expression thundered. "Don't like to think of you hitching yourself to that disagreeable Brockton."

"He's never been disagreeable to me," Caro said. "Quite the opposite."

The coach lurched to a stop, and a footman raced to open the door and assist them from the vehicle.

A light snow was falling.

Inside the Elizabethan entry hall paneled with age-darkened wood, the ancient Aldridge butler greeted the sisters he'd known since the day of their birth.

Caro handed off her muffler and cloak. "Tell me, Barrow, who has arrived."

"His and her grace are here, and Lord and

Lady Haverstock arrived about an hour ago. The dowagers Haverstock and Finchley came rather earlier. And there's a Lord Broughton."

He hadn't adulterated Lord Brockton's name too badly. "Then the Rothcomb-Smedleys haven't arrived yet?" Margaret said almost in a shout because poor Barrow had a propensity to mangle Clair's married name— to Clair's consternation. He used to call her distinguished husband Mr. Rotten-Smelly.

He shook his white-topped head. "Not yet, my lady."

"What about Mr. and Mrs. Morgan?" Margaret asked, also speaking much more loudly than normal.

"Oh, yes, they came with the Haverstocks. Your servants, too, have all arrived and taken your things to your chambers, and your brother plans on dinner at five."

She would barely have time to change from her traveling clothes. It was important to her that she look fetching.

She meant to win a proposal of marriage from the Earl of Brockton before Christmas.

$\mathcal{C}$hapter 3

Caro peered into her looking glass before going down to dinner and was assured that she could not have projected a prettier appearance. Her hair was artfully arranged in a swept-up style, and her pale blue gown that was almost sheer enough to see through displayed her figure—which she knew to be fine—to great advantage.

Downstairs, they went into the dining chamber, where the long table had been reduced to seat tonight's dozen. The room was ablaze with candlelight from three glittering chandeliers and a pair of fine silver candelabra—a gift to the fourth duke from Charles II.

She was chagrined that her brother had not seated her near Lord Brockton. A frown on her face, she took her place. At her right was Lord Haverstock, who sat next to her brother, and his plain but entertaining sister Lydia was at her left. The object of Caro's attentions sat across the table, two places down.

One might blame the duchess for the seating arrangements, but Caro knew that sweet-tempered Elizabeth would always adhere to her husband's preferences on such a matter. It was no secret that Aldridge was not fond of a union between his sister and the rakish Lord Brockton.

Caro need not have been concerned. From the moment they took their places, she felt Lord Brockton's eyes upon her. Recalling the early days of her . . . her relationship with Mr. Perry, she remembered how aggressive she had been. Aggression was what was called for tonight.

She smiled down the table at him. He really was terribly handsome. Fashionably cut cork-coloured hair framed his uncommonly handsome face with its lichen-coloured eyes and a nose that was almost conspicuous for its perfection.

When their gazes met, her lashes lowered seductively. "I trust your lordship's room was satisfactory?" How silly of her to refer to him as your lordship when three of the five gentlemen at the table could answer to that title.

"It's quite lovely."

His eyes raked over her from the top of her golden tresses to settle on her bosom. Her cheeks stung as if she were standing in front of him perfectly naked.

"And your journey, Lord Brockton?" she asked.

"Most satisfactory—except for the wretched

cold."

The duchess addressed him. "Which I hope will make our home all the more welcome. We have such fine wood fires in the country." She looked at the fire blazing not eight feet away.

"Indeed, your grace," Lord Brockton said. "My chamber was most welcoming. As warm as toast."

Elizabeth nodded. "We sent ahead, asking for fires in every chamber, and we are fortunate to have wonderfully competent servants."

Lord Brockton directed his next comment to Caro. "I do hope you were not too cold on your journey, Lady Caroline."

"I will own it was rather frigid, but that only made Glenmont more welcoming." She sighed, never losing her smile. "I cannot imagine being anywhere else at Christmas." Once more, she looked into his eyes as if they were the only two people in the chamber. "We are so pleased that you could join us, Lord Brockton."

"The pleasure is all mine."

Though the room was well lit, he alone was in partial shadow. Something about the darkness slashing his face accentuated his rugged handsomeness. She could not help but admire how fine a face he possessed with its deeply cleft chin and aristocratic nose.

Throughout the dinner, every time her gaze went to that part of the table, he was watching her. That he found her attractive was most probable; that her dowry contributed to her desirability was certain. He would offer for her by Christmas. By the Epiphany, she could be Lady Brockton with a fine home on Grosvenor Square and a husband who was considered the most handsome man in the Capital. Which was exactly what she wanted.

Well, not exactly, but it would suffice. She had seen enough marriages between noble houses to know that once lives were intertwined, love often came. By next Christmas she should be madly in love with Lord Brockton.

Perhaps not as madly as she had loved Christopher Perry, but she mustn't allow herself to dwell on her unfortunate alliance with a man who had no intention of ever marrying her. Mr. Perry was her past. Lord Brockton was her future.

Something inside of her softened. Could she be a mother this time next year?

"May I pour you claret, Lady Caroline?" Lord Haverstock asked.

"Yes, thank you, my lord."

Caro peered down the table at Lady Haverstock. It was a wonder Lord Brockton could train his gaze on Caro when Haverstock's exquisite dark-haired wife graced their table. That lady's porcelain perfect face was dominated by huge almond-shaped eyes the colour of rich coffee beans. It was impossible not to stare at her stunning beauty.

Caro's gaze shifted to Lord Haverstock's sister. "Why, Lady Lydia, are you not eating?"

Before Lydia could respond, her mother did. "My daughter is one of those unfortunate women who actually grows thinner when she's increasing."

"My poor Lyddie's been wretchedly sick," said Morgie.

Lord Finchley, who sat next to Mr. Morgan, eyed his neighbor's plate. "I say, Morgie, it looks as if you're not eating, either."

"Sadly, that is true. One would think it was my husband who's breeding." Lydia pushed the French beans around the crested plate with the tines of her fork. "It was the same when we were expecting our son. Morgie was so nervous and upset about me, he couldn't eat."

These comments apparently embarrassed Morgie, who was eager to change the topic of conversation. He turned to Lord Finchley. "I say, Finch, is your friend Perry coming? Capital fellow!"

All eyes—except Lord Finchley's—darted to Lord Brockton.

Lord Finchley glared at Caro. "No, he's spending Christmas with his own family." Lord Finchley spoke without his usual gayety. No doubt he was as displeased as Margaret that Caro was terminating her fruitless relationship with Mr. Perry. Could none of them understand her hair could silver, and still there would be no proposal from him?

Caro was not a dreamer like Margaret. She was a pragmatist.

Her gaze went to Lord Brockton. His lips folded into a grim line.

Good. He was jealous of Mr. Perry.

"A pity." Morgie's brows lowered as he peered across the table at Caro. "I expect Lady Caroline's disappointed."

Silence filled the chamber like a death pall.

"Not in the least," she finally said. She then glanced at Lord Brockton, her eyes flashing and a coy smile upon her face.

Amusement danced in his mossy green eyes.

* * *

After the men had imbibed their port, they entered the drawing room where Caro was quick to pounce upon her brother. She dare not wait until he was seated. If she made her request in front of the other men, good manners would dictate that he not deny her. "My dearest brother, I beg that you allow me to give Lord Brockton a tour of Glenmont."

Aldridge stiffened, but only one who had known him her entire life would realize the rigidity of his demeanor. He hesitated a moment before responding. "You may, but don't be long. We'll be wanting to form whist tables."

Surely he didn't think she would allow Lord Brockton to ravish her! One who had denied the man she had loved long and passionately was not likely to fling herself at a man who'd yet to make her heartbeat race. She gave a bitter laugh. Even the thought of Christopher Perry still had the power to accelerate her heartbeat.

Aldridge nodded, then directed his attention to his wife.

Lord Brockton offered his arm, and they crossed the Turkey carpet and swept through the doorway into a long, wooden corridor which ran from the east side of the house to the west.

If she had been a fresh debutante, Aldridge would never have permitted her to be alone with a known rake. But she not only was not a young miss fresh from the schoolroom, she was no longer young. She was humiliated over Mr. Perry's failure to propose marriage. She must be the laughing stock of the *ton*—a duke's daughter incapable of coaxing a declaration from her longtime suitor—a man whose own origins should make him honored to wed into the Ponsby/Aldridge family.

"I daresay your ancestral home is great deal finer than our discordant pile," she said playfully.

"Piedmorton is not nearly as large as Glenmont. How many chambers have you here?" He covered her hand which rested on his sleeve.

"I'm not sure anyone knows. Aldridge says two hundred and sixteen, but I daresay he accounts a china closet to be a chamber. God only knows how he came up with the number."

"Will we see all of them tonight?" he asked.

She shook her head. "No, only the ones on this floor. That will be quite enough."

She led him to a large chamber with wood-beamed ceilings soaring high above. "This was once the great hall, I expect during Tudor times, but it's now our armory."

He began to stroll the perimeter of the vast room, peering with interest at the various crossed swords and axes adorning the gray stone walls and the suits of armor standing as if ready to do battle. He stood next to one. "Would you say I'm a great deal taller than your ancestors who wore these?"

She smiled playfully. "Let me see . . ." She knew very well he was a great deal taller. Was he fishing for a compliment? "It's difficult to say since the top of the helmet is level with the top of your head, my lord." Her gaze skimmed his broad shoulders. "However, as this man's shoulders hit your chest, I would say you're considerably taller. I will point out that my brother Aldridge is also a great deal taller so it looks as if the family must have married into height."

He chuckled.

He dropped his hand from hers and spent far more time than she would have preferred pausing to examine each weapon, each set of armor with the eager interest of a young lad. "Ah, to have lived in the day where the lord of the land led his men into battle!"

"I daresay in actuality it wouldn't have been anything to glory about. It's not as if one would cheer when his brother was thwacked in half."

When she could finally manage to remove him from the armory, she quickly led him through the warren of rooms heavily paneled in dark old oak and furnished with big, chunky pieces of equally dark furniture.

The last room she came to was the library. She paused in front of a tall door of darkened oak and opened it. "This is the library. Aldridge rather hoards it to himself. Always working here on Parliamentary affairs." She moved to stand in front of the chimneypiece where a fire roared. How their conscientious servants managed to add logs and stoke the fires without ever being seen was a mystery to her. The winter fires at Glenmont never waned until all the guests were fast asleep in their beds.

He moved next to her. "You mentioned Piedmorton. I should like to bring you there, Caroline." His voice was husky, his hand pressing hers in a slow, circular motion.

Besides her brothers, no man had ever called her Caroline. Except for Christopher. Once—the night she had allowed him to press his lips to her breasts in Lady Melbourne's garden. Her breath became erratic at the memory. How she had wanted to lie with him that night! She might have, too, had he not suddenly become strangely formal.

Lord Brockton was practically proposing to her. Was that not what she wanted? Why, then, was she not being her usual coquettish self and offering him encouragement? Why, when he had used her first name so intimately, had she not felt at least a fraction of the thrill she had when Christopher did?

This man is my future.

"I should adore seeing Piedmorton," she answered in a much more lighthearted tone than he had used.

He came closer. His hands clasped her shoulders and he lowered his head to settle his lips upon hers.

Her first instinct was to back away. That was how she had acted when gentlemen had attempted to kiss her in the years between her come out and her capitulation to Mr. Perry's charms. Whenever a man had previously wanted to kiss her, she had pushed him away. Before Christopher, when she became the aggressor.

Now she needed to coax herself into moving into Lord Brockton's arms with the same fluidity she had with her former lover. Now she must endeavor to infuse passion into this kiss.

She forced herself to relax as he kissed her. She forced herself to press closer to him as his arms came around her. A pity she could not force herself to enjoy the kiss, to breathe the same lustfulness into it that she always had with Christopher's kisses.

That will come.

Long after the kiss, he stood there holding her in his arms before the fire. "My dearest Caroline, you must realize how greatly I hold you in esteem, how devotedly I love you, how thoroughly I want to make your my wife."

Even though this was exactly what she'd been planning, it had come so fast she was not prepared when it actually happened. She had thought he would spend at least two or three days getting to know her before he declared himself.

Her stomach clenched. Her chest tightened. *This is my future.* Her entire future depended upon how she would respond to him. Once she assented to marry him, she would never again be held in Christopher's arms. All faint hope of becoming Christopher's wife would die.

"I should be honored, my lord."

"Then I'll speak to your brother."

No! Aldridge's only request when consenting to invite Lord Brockton was that she not make any hasty decisions. As it was, her brother was not disposed to admire the earl. She must see to it that over the next few days Lord Brockton was displayed in a favorable manner. "I beg that you wait. I am of age. I will marry you. May we announce our betrothal on Christmas Day?"

"Whatever my beloved wants." His spine straightened and he looked as proud as a prince of the blood. "I pity I can't slay a dragon between now and Christmas to impress your brother."

This fellow obviously wished to have been born in an earlier, less civilized time. She raised a hand. "Gentleman-like behavior will go much further with my brother than bloodshed, " she said with a laugh. "Come, let's join the others."

"I request to have you as my whist partner."

"One should be able to learn a lot about another person by playing whist with that person."

" I beg you not put too much importance upon skill at whist. Bear in mind that I've not spent much time at a whist table. As a bachelor, I've had many other pursuits. I assure you my skill at whist will improve with experience."

As the races at Newmarket, faro at White's, and dallying with ladies of the stage no doubt claimed his attentions. She could well believe he'd spent little time seated at a whist table.

After they joined the others and went to their respective tables, she learned that he'd spoken the truth about his deficiencies at the game.

* * *

The following afternoon as the ladies—with the exception of the dowagers—were walking the long gallery, speaking animatedly, and peering at the carpet of snow outside the many windows, a coach entered the long drive to the house, and each lady's gaze followed its progression up the ribbon of a lane.

"I expect that's the Rothcomb-Smedleys," the duchess said.

But as the coach came closer, Caro realized it was not their sister's coach. It was an exceptionally fine carriage, much finer than the one Claire and her husband used. In fact, it looked very much like Mr. Perry's coach.

Her heartbeat began to roar at the very contemplation. A lamentable and uncontrollable habit.

"I don't think it's our sister," Margaret said, pausing to narrow her eyes and peer through the mullions framed with snow drifts.

By the time the carriage came to the front courtyard, Caro remarked dryly, "It's Mr. Perry."

$\mathcal{C}$hapter 4

Several times during the long, frigid coach ride from London, Christopher had given serious thought to ordering that his carriage turn back. What the devil was he doing going to Glenmont? Would the duke turn up his nose at him? Or, worse yet, turn him away?

He shouldn't go. Even if Finch *had* invited him, and Finch *was* a member of the powerful Aldridge/Haverstock clan by virtue of marrying the duke's sister.

He really hated to let Finch down, though. Finch wouldn't have invited Christopher if his presence would not have been welcome.

Christopher's friendship with Finch was of such long standing that everyone thought of them as brothers. No two brothers could be closer than he and the Earl of Finchley. Since neither he nor Finch had a brother, they did serve as such to one another.

For the past year, he'd resisted every invitation from Lady Caroline to visit her family's ancestral home. Being her guest might display an intimacy he was not prepared to confirm. He'd come once before for the baptism of the Rothcomb-Smedleys' daughter, but he'd been Finch's guest and returned to London the same day.

Why, then, had he allowed himself to come today? He most certainly had not changed his mind about marrying her. He supposed he was coming out of fear—fear that Caroline would unite herself to so unworthy a man as Lord Brockton.

Even at the expense of his own humiliation, he must do everything in his power to stop her from marrying Brockton.

Everything but offering for her himself.

His first glimpse of Glenmont today brought to mind how surprised he'd been when he first saw it. Glenmont was not at all one of those grand, palatial homes other dukes, like the Duke of Marlborough, lived in. It was as different from Blenheim Palace as St. Christopher's huge domed church in the heart of London was to a country chapel. Not that Glenmont was small. It rambled over a considerable amount of property, yet something about it was humble. Portions of it were still timbered. Others were of local stone with small, mullioned windows. No huge Palladian windows on this old family home.

Its lack of opulence helped to sooth his nervousness.

When he stepped into the wood-paneled entry hall, he realized his entry onto the property had not gone unnoticed. Several of the family members came to greet him. Finch's wife curtsied first, then said, "I must go to the billiards room and tell John you've come! He'll be so excited." With that, she took off down a long, narrow corridor.

That left him with the Duchess of Aldridge and her sister Lady Lydia—*and Lady Caroline*. He bowed first to the duchess, then to her sister, and lastly, he faced Caroline. Even when he'd first met her, he'd not been this nervous. He'd spent years cultivating his reputation as a well-heeled, well-educated ladies' man who was welcome in the best circles. He had become accustomed to women throwing themselves at his feet. Indeed, even those first early days of his . . . friendship with her, it had been she who was the aggressor.

There was something about her that made her stand out from other lovely ladies of the *haute ton*—and it wasn't that she was a duke's daughter.

He felt that same indefinable attraction today as he peered at her. He wished she hadn't worn that soft blue frock that clung to her smooth curves and never failed to arouse him. Her slight and fair blonde beauty was upstaged by the sensuousness of a courtesan she exuded whenever they were together. He had felt it in those earliest days of their acquaintance, and he felt it now. Her desirability was as palpable as his own heartbeat. His head inclined. "Lady Caroline."

"You've brought your mother?" she asked, her gaze flicking to the outer door.

He shook his head. "No."

"But Lord Finchley said you could not leave her at Christmas."

It was good that Finch had told the group of his invitation. He felt less of an interloper. "Actually, she left me. We received a communication early this morning that my next-to-eldest sister's time had come, and she was calling for Mama to come be with her at the birth of her first child."

"Then it's to be a Christmas baby," the duchess exclaimed.

He shrugged. "It's my belief my sister will not be able to wait until Christmas."

"We are most happy that you've come to us," the duchess said.

Funny, he'd never been uncomfortable in the presence of the duchess, but her husband was another story. The man's air of complete authority intimidated Christopher.

"We were strolling in the gallery when we saw your coach come up the drive," Caroline said. "You're welcome to join us, but I daresay you'd rather be with the men."

"Indeed he would," said Finch, strolling into the hall with a huge smile on his face. "So you changed your mind after all. Devilishly happy to have you. Have you brought your mother?"

Christopher explained about Susan's babe.

Then he saw Brockton. The man did not look happy. Why had he even left the billiard room? Surely Brockton hadn't come here to greet him. It wasn't as if they were friends. The scoundrel ought to have realized that Christopher had snubbed him when he left White's two nights ago. More likely he meant to interfere with any possible communication between Christopher and Caroline.

He moved closer to Christopher. In an attempt to suppress his hostile expression, Brockton offered a bow and effected a smile that was as friendly as a viper. "So, Perry, you've come to celebrate Christmas with us. I didn't know those of your faith shared in our celebration."

Christopher stiffened, but before he could respond, Caroline stepped forward and addressed the obnoxious man in a hostile voice. "Mr. Perry's a Christian."

The duchess came and linked her arm in Christopher's. "We are delighted you've come, Mr. Perry. Once my husband's sister Claire arrives, our party will be complete." With him at her side, she began to mount the stairs, and the others followed. "This will be the greatest Christmas ever."

* * *

Lord Brockton came to offer his arm to Caro, who was following the duchess upstairs to the drawing room. "I know it's wickedly cold outside," he said, "but nothing would make me happier than to take a sleigh ride with you at my side and both of us tucked beneath a fur rug."

She laughed. "It sounds far more romantic than it would feel. I daresay you haven't seen how fierce the wind is today. We would be miserable."

Truth to tell, she wasn't yet ready to be alone with the man. He was sure to want to kiss her again, and she did not enjoy it in the least. Her insides clenched. Why did Christopher Perry have to intrude into her courtship with Lord Brockton? If she hadn't seen him today—and been instantly and intensely attracted to him as she always was—she might have better warmed to Lord Brockton—her future.

Christopher Perry is my past. She vowed to ignore him during the remainder of his stay. It would be difficult, given that everything about him—his every expression, the timbre of his deep voice, the obsidian flash in his simmering eyes—was stamped into her memory as if they'd been branded with a hot iron.

She allowed herself to gaze at Lord Brockton's profile. A pity his handsomeness failed to accelerate her heartbeat. She sighed and patted his arm possessively. She'd always longed to belong to someone. And now she would belong to this man. That thought pleased her. That and the knowledge she'd be mistress of her own house.

In the drawing room, her breath caught at the sight of Christopher Perry, who stood near the chimneypiece. All the draperies were open to let into the chamber the day's waning light—too gray to be called sunshine. She sat on a rose silken settee with Lord Brockton beside her.

Her thoughts were still on his Grosvenor Square house. She was eager to see its interior. Would it measure up to Mr. Perry's? Some said Christopher Perry's house was the finest in London. She agreed. For more than a year she had believed she would one day be its mistress.

Now she knew she never would.

A moment later the duke entered the chamber with Lord Haverstock and Mr. Morgan, and they all stood. The duke went straight to Mr. Perry. "How good of you to come, Perry. Your presence will help to make this the most joyous Christmas ever."

As the duke went to take his seat on the throne-like chair that matched the one Christopher sat in, Caro pondered her brother's friendly greeting to her *former* lover. In nearly two years of acquaintance, Aldridge had never before been so amiable to him. The only explanation for it was her brother's intense dislike of Lord Brockton.

It was imperative for her future happiness

that this man to whom she was betrothed ingratiate himself to her brother. But what heroic acts could he possibly perform to redeem himself in Aldridge's eyes? She would have to ponder it.

They heard a great fuss being made downstairs amidst door slamming. "I daresay the Rothcomb-Smedleys have finally arrived," Lord Haverstock said.

He was proven correct minutes later when Claire and her husband entered the drawing room. Greetings were exchanged, then Claire sat by Margaret, and her husband took a seat to Lord Haverstock's right. All the men in the chamber—except Lord Brockton, who took no interest in politics—launched into a discussion of Parliamentary matters.

Even Mr. Morgan, who formerly eschewed governmental matters, had successfully stood for the House of Commons this past year and was turning out to be a promising legislator. All the men in the family claimed he understood budgetary matters better than any of them. He'd diligently trimmed government waste and had even managed to withhold an increase in the Regent's Civil List.

Caro turned to her betrothed and whispered, "Excuse me. I've just remembered something."

It was impossible for her to think when others were talking. She needed solitude. She must return to the long gallery. Walking alone was the only way she could clear her mind enough to help devise a plan to restore Lord Brockton's honor—at least in her brother's eyes.

* * *

Aldridge's friendly greeting came as such a shock. Christopher had thought perhaps the duke was playing a cruel hoax upon him. He froze and gazed into the lofty peer's dark eyes. The amiability in Aldridge's smiling face and in his voice was genuine.

To further expand his rare friendliness, the duke even sat at the chair directly opposite Christopher's and engaged him in conversation. "Allow me to say—and I know I also speak for Lord Haverstock—we were mightily impressed when you stood for Parliament and put the vast Perry resources behind your efforts. I wish we had a hundred of you. Isn't that so, Haverstock?"

The marquess nodded. "Just so long as they continue voting with the Whigs."

Surely his mediocre success in the House of Commons did not account for this sudden befriending by the Duke of Aldridge. Christopher shrugged. "I follow Lord Finchley, and Lord Finchley follows the two of you."

Throughout the course of his adult life, Christopher had learned that when another man suddenly warmed to him that other man usually wanted to tap into Christopher's exceptional wealth. But that could not explain the Duke of Aldridge's reversal of stiffness this afternoon. It was an acknowledged fact that Aldridge was one of the wealthiest aristocrats in all of England.

What then? Why had the duke taken it upon himself to treat Christopher with something so akin to affection?

"With the election of you and Mr. Morgan this year and the addition of Finchley to the House of Lords, we've gained three votes," Aldridge said, smiling.

Smiling! The man had never before smiled at him.

Then Aldridge's eyes narrowed as his gaze moved to Lord Brockton. "Why, Brockton, do you not serve in the House of Lords?"

The scoundrel hesitated a moment before responding. "Alas, your grace, I've been too busy."

"At Newmarket?" Aldridge glared at Brockton with a far more stern demeanor than he had ever directed at Christopher. Could it be the duke did not look favorably upon a union between Brockton and his sister? The duke was acting like a suspicious father who wished to eliminate his daughter's unsavory suitors.

Now Christopher understood. Aldridge clearly did *not* approve of Brockton as a potential husband for Lady Caroline. He was so opposed to the union, he was willing to give the illusion that he'd rather pledge Caroline to the great grandson of a Jewish jeweler than permit her to wed the wicked Lord Brockton. Of course, Christopher was merely a handy stand-in rival. Not a *real* rival. What duke would have his sister marry so far beneath her?

"As I'm maturing," Lord Brockton said to the duke, "I've come to see that my sense of duty is calling me to serve in the House of Lords. Men like us—peers of the realm—need to lead the country."

The liar! Not a month ago Christopher had heard him at White's telling his drunken friends he had no intentions of ever sitting through dull sessions of Parliament when he could be bedding opera dancers or going to the race meetings.

Christopher had no desire to listen while these men discussed Parliament. Emblazoned on his brain like corrosive acid was the vision of that unworthy scoundrel sitting so close on the cozy settee with Lady Caroline Ponsby. It was more destructive than sword slashes on a Michelangelo canvas. Nothing could be more wrong!

How he wanted to be that man seated beside her. For the rest of their lives.

But that could never be.

* * *

Because of all the windows, this gallery was the coldest room in the big, rambling house. For warmth, she forced herself to walk briskly, and though she warmed some, she wished she'd taken the time to fetch a shawl.

Taking long, quick strides, she analyzed her brother's perspective. He obviously thought Lord Brockton a wastrel fortune hunter who would squander her considerable dowry on gaming and shameless women. Her heart sank. What if that proved to be his intentions? Surely he must be attracted to her. Men always had been.

She refused to think such uncharitable thoughts.

Instead, she put her mind to devising a scheme to improve her brother's opinion of Lord Brockton. First, Lord Brockton must vow to take his seat in the House of Lords. Her brother was passionate about his Whig politics, and the more like-minded men who served with him, the happier he would be.

Other than his love of Parliamentary duties, her brother's other passions were for his wife, whom he adored, and their toddler son, Ram—the Marquess of Ramsbury, who was the light of his father's eyes.

She would have to advise Lord Brockton to be effusive in his praise of Elizabeth and Ram. Aldridge would positively glow.

Would these things be enough to win her brother's approval?

She sighed. Even though she was old enough to marry without her brother's consent, she did not want to do so. Theirs was and always had been a close family, and she did not ever want to do something that would estrange her from them.

If only Lord Brockton could slay the metaphoric dragon! She pondered this a moment. Perhaps there was a way. What if she could stage a situation in which little Ram appeared to be in danger, and at great personal risk, Lord Brockton saved the little boy?

But what kind of danger? A charging bull? A fall from a great height? A snatching by wicked highwaymen? Any of these, of course, could not actually threaten her precious nephew.She was giving this considerable consideration when a door creaked open. She spun around to see who had entered the gallery.

His face bathed in the yellow glow of a wall sconce, Christopher Perry strolled toward her.

$\mathcal{C}$hapter 5

Christopher had waited to take his leave until the duke was forcing Brockton into a discussion on the merits of serving in the House of Lords. Then he quietly slipped away. If Lady Caroline had gone to her bedchamber, she would have bid goodbye to the group. She must be either on this floor or on the ground floor.

A pity it was such a vast, rambling house. He might never find her. He descended the broad wooden staircase to the ground floor and strolled along a long corridor, peering into each chamber he passed. What had she been doing when he arrived? Hadn't someone mentioned that the ladies had been walking the gallery whilst the gentlemen played billiards?

Perhaps she meant to return there to fetch something like her shawl. He wasn't precisely sure where the gallery was in this rambling house, but he recalled that they'd been able to observe his entrance, so he knew it must be on the south side. He turned back and walked along the east-west corridor.

And he found her. She turned around and

glared at him when he entered the chamber. How lovely she looked in the gossamer sky blue gown that skimmed along the smooth curves her body. His throat went dry as he gazed upon her.

"What are you doing here?" she snapped.

He moved toward her. "I'm not really sure. I suppose I was concerned about you."

"No need to be." She did not look at him when she issued her harsh response. It was if she were hell bent on strolling this frigid chamber—and ignoring him.

He would not be dissuaded. He fell into step beside her and saw that she trembled from the cold. "You're wrong. I do have reason to be concerned. Dressed so flimsily, you'll take lung fever. Can I not persuade you to come to a warmer room?"

She shook her head. "I can only concentrate on matters when I walk. Alone."

"Then allow me to fetch your shawl." What she really needed was a fur-lined cape and leather gloves.

"If I walk fast enough, it will heat me."

"You're being obstinate."

"You're being rude, infringing on my desired solitude."

He shook his head. "It's you who's being rude. One should not run off from one's guests."

"I suppose I am being rude."

"What is this matter of great import that

you're pondering?"

"It's a private matter."

"Does it have to do with Brockton?"

"Perhaps."

"I would not be your friend if I didn't warn you that he's not the sort of man who will ever value a lady."

"I know that he's a reputed rake who seeks to wed an heiress." She came to the wall, turned, and continued on at her fast pace.

He wished he could reveal to her that Brockton had boasted that he'd keep his lowborn mistress if he married Lady Caroline, but no gentleman would ever repeat so tawdry a tale to a lady. Instead, he said, "He's worse than that. He's a vile man who's barely tolerated in polite circles."

Her mouth folded into a grim line and her pace quickened. Her satin slippers slapped along the cold, marble floors. Slap, slap, slap, slap, pivot at the wall, slap, slap, slap, slap, pivot at the wall. Repeat. All the while she ignored him as if he were one of the portraits lining the chamber's cold stone walls.

Despite the briskness of her walk, she had not warmed. Her skin tinged a milky blue, and her teeth chattered like bottles in a speeding buggy. He truly feared she *would* make herself sick. When he could stand it no longer, he yanked off his own jacket.

She stopped. Her eyes widened as they raked over his upper torso, then for the first time since he'd entered the gallery ten minutes earlier, she looked him in the eye. "What are you doing?"

He moved to her and draped his coat over her shoulders, pulling it together just below her chin. "I cannot be a party to your self-destruction." *In more ways than this.*

She twisted as if to free herself of his coat, but he continued to clasp it in front of her. "You, my lady, have two choices. You can shed my jacket and move to a warmer room, or you can continue here—wearing my jacket."

Anger flashed across her face. "You're the one who's obstinate."

He moved closer, peered down into her face, and spoke throatily. "We've always been alike, Caroline." And in spite of their divergent origins, they *were* alike. Perhaps that's why they'd always been drawn to one another. Their similarities extended to that indefinable sensuousness that flared in both of them every time they'd been together.

Even now, even in this chilly chamber, there was a feverish look on her face when their eyes locked. He'd come to know her every expression, every nuance in her body. Her breath silently hitched, as it always did when they were this close.

He let down his guard and reached out to stroke her face. She took advantage of his lapse to try to wiggle out of his jacket. "You're not to address me so familiarly," she snapped. "I am Lady Caroline to you."

Her words were like a slap in his face. He wanted to protest, to remind her of the intimacies they had shared, but he remained mute as he gazed solemnly at the woman he loved. There had been times over this past year and half when she had slipped and called him by his first name. The very memory of his name spoken softly on her kissable lips had the power to accelerate his breathing.

But he could not dredge up what had been, not when he was unwilling to advance the relationship. "Forgive me," he said somberly.

She shoved the jacket back at him. "Pray, Mr. Perry, do restore your clothing. This is most improper."

And so it was. "Why is it you bring out the improper in me, *Lady* Caroline?"

Their eyes locked again. She was the first to flick away. "Will you tell me something?"

"Yes."

"Why when all the times I begged you to come to Glenmont, you refused, and now, when I don't want you here, you show up?"

These words were far worse than a slap in the face. *She doesn't want me here.* His humiliation was insignificant compared to the rip that tore through his heart. He'd always known she would find someone more worthy of her love than he. He just hadn't been prepared for that day to come so soon. And he would never be able to accept that she could give herself to the most unworthy man in the kingdom.

"I've already explained. I came because I care too much for you to ever see you unite yourself to someone not fit to be in the same room with you."

"I pray you're not referring to Lord Brockton," she said coolly.

He came closer and said in a low, husky voice. "You know I do."

"I wish you wouldn't. Lord Brockton has always been all that's amiable to me. He has much to recommend him. Do you not agree that he's incredibly handsome?"

Christopher shrugged. "How should I know if a man's handsome?"

"He does have other attributes. He's a peer of the realm, and he's got a fine country house as well as a grand mansion on Grosvenor Square."

His anger simmered. "You've seen these places?"

"Not yet."

"You've kissed him?"

"Of course," she said flippantly.

A singeing fury crashed over him with shocking potency. Until this moment he'd not thought of her actually *kissing* another man. No woman's kisses had ever affected him as profoundly as hers. Surely she couldn't have kissed that blighter in the same way she'd kissed him!

He eyed her and swallowed hard. He wasn't certain if he wanted to know the truth, but some strange force compelled him to ask. "Can you honestly tell me you kissed him in the same way you kissed me?"

Their gazes connected as if by forging iron. She drew a wobbly breath. "Are you saying that I kissed you in a certain way, Mr. Perry?"

He hated this wall of formality she'd erected between them. His anger ignited a most *informal* response.

In one long stride he reached her, firmly clasped her shoulders, and pulled her to him for a hungry kiss.

Little ripples of pleasure ran through her, and her breath became labored. His arms came fully around her as she molded to his body like clay. Her mouth opened beneath the pressure of his.

He was as profoundly affected by the searing kiss as she.

The door to the chamber banged open.

They looked up to see Lord Brockton standing there, his legs spread apart and fury blazing on his face. "What in the hell do you think you're doing with my betrothed?"

Caroline stepped away from him, fear etched on her face as she regarded the swine, Brockton.

Christopher met her frightened gaze. "Is this true? Are you betrothed to Lord

Brockton?"

Her eyes filled with tears, and she slowly nodded.

Chapter 6

Her face flamed, her watery gaze dropped to the floor. Christopher then excused himself with two words. "Forgive me." He said this not to Brockton but to her, and then he raced from the room. It had not only been the most awkward moment of his life. It was also the most horrifying.

The announcement of Caroline's betrothal was as shocking and painful as the death of a loved one. Indeed, the only time he'd ever felt like this was when his father died suddenly at the age of two and forty.

His heartbeat roaring, he paced from one long wooden corridor to another. During his anger-fueled walk, inky skies replaced the day's fading light. He easily outpaced the aged butler, who was lumbering along, lighting the sconces at fifteen-foot intervals.

His initial humiliation at Lady Caroline's rejection quickly melted away. Even though she told him she didn't want him at Glenmont, even though she had foolishly accepted Brockton's offer, even though he could never be worthy of Caroline, he would not surrender and allow the most offensive man he'd ever known to ruin the life of the woman he loved.

Were it not for the breathless passion of their kiss, he might have been forced to capitulate. But a woman in love with her betrothed would not have kissed another man as Caroline had just done. Just remembering it caused him to groan with want of her.

She cannot throw herself away on such a scoundrel! He was comforted in the knowledge that her powerful brother felt the same. Now he and the duke had two things in common. Now that Christopher had finally followed in his father's footsteps and successfully stood for the House of Commons, they shared political interests. More importantly, he and the duke bitterly opposed a marriage between Lady Caro and the blackguard earl.

Finch, whose wife's favorite sister was Lady Caroline, had already expressed his horror at the thought of being forced to welcome Brockton into their family.

The pity of it was that Lady Caroline was of age. She could very well wed the scoundrel without her brother's permission. By marrying Finch in that manner, her sister had set the example. Christopher was determined to enlist the duke and Finch to crush Brockton's hopes.

* * *

Caro was frightened at the fury in Lord

Brockton's flashing eyes as he moved to her after Christopher left the gallery. "So you had an assignation with your former lover." His lips sneered. He spoke harshly.

"No. I came here to think. I wanted to come up with a list of things you could do to ingratiate yourself with my brother. I don't know how Mr. Perry found me."

"You certainly gave him a warm welcome." There was contempt in his voice.

She shook her head. "I told him I didn't even want him at Glenmont."

"Yet the man was disrobing."

"I . . . I was very cold. He . . . forced his coat upon me. To warm me."

He moved closer, his gaze simmering. "From now on, your kisses will only be for me." His voice was husky as he crushed her to him and kissed her bruisingly.

The kiss was nothing like Christopher's. And certainly her reaction to it was nothing like her reaction had been to Christopher's excruciatingly tender kiss. Then, her lids had gently lowered and her lips easily parted. Every second had been pleasurable.

Unlike now. All she could think of was how uncomfortable her neck was, how unpleasant was the pressure of his lips on hers, the burn from his stubble, the stale smell of yesterday's brandy. She felt no more desire for this man than she did for the man driving the carriage.

She consoled herself, though. *I am finally betrothed! I will no longer be a spinster. I will be mistress of my own home.* And, lastly, she would become a mother. Once her life was intertwined with this man's, love would come.

Her heartbeat caught when she thought of Lord Haverstock's sister Mrs. Reeves' unhappy marriage. But that woman had not desired love. She had desired the rank she thought Mr. Reeves would inherit when his ducal uncle died.

Caroline would endeavor to create a loving home with this man who now held her in his arms. She wanted to fall in love with him.

When he finally pulled away, he asked, "So what am I to do to win your brother's approval—other than serving in the House of Lords, which I've already vowed to do?"

"First, he needs to be assured you won't squander away my dowry. Therefore, you must convince him that your interest in gaming has waned."

His brows raised. "So how much is you dowry?"

She shrugged. "Each of my sisters received thirty thousand, so I assume I shall also. Unless I have to wed without his approval. In that case, I might not have a dowry."

"I must ensure that your brother approves of me." A huge smile spread across his face. "How fortunate I am to have won the hand of the loveliest lady in London—as well as thirty thousand. I don't mind telling you I need it most desperately."

"Not, I hope, because of gaming losses?"

He nodded ruefully. "But I will be a changed man."

Was he telling the truth? She wished she better knew the man's character. "You must also realize that while my brother is most devoted to his younger siblings, the light of his life is in his wife and their young son, the Marquess of Ramsbury. We call the adorable lad Ram."

"So I'm to show uncommon respect to the duchess and effusively praise the lad?"

"Yes. I'm trying to work out the details where you will become my brother's hero by saving his son's life, but it needs to be something that would in no way jeopardize my nephew's safety."

He gave a wicked smile. "Oh, I like this. . ."

* * *

That night at dinner, Christopher was pleased to be seated next to Lady Caroline. He was not pleased that she ignored him throughout the meal. She directed pleasantries to all those around her. All those except for him. She obviously wanted to demonstrate to her betrothed that there was nothing between her and Christopher.

She might also wish to demonstrate to Christopher her anger over their stolen kiss. Her displeasure over the kiss was almost as devastating as the knowledge that she had agreed to wed Brockton. Since the day of their first scorching kiss, Caroline had schemed to be alone with him whenever she could. She had thrived on their passionate kisses.

He could still feel her pliant body pressed against his, still feel the languid stroke of her tongue on his, still hear her whimpering as he held her in his arms. How painful it was for him to recall.

He had to purge her from his thoughts. His attention turned to the foot of the table where the duchess was speaking with Finch's grandmother. Because the dowager was so fond of her only grandchild, her affections were also lavished on his friends. She was the first lady of the nobility who had ever treated him as if he were her grandson's equal. She'd always included him in their family gatherings—almost as if he were one of their distinguished family.

Even though Brockton was at the other end of the table, his attention also went to the duchess, and his loud voice carried like Kean's upon the stage at Drury Lane. "Forgive me, your grace, if I keep staring at you," Brockton said to the duchess, "but your beauty quite robs me of breath. Aldridge is indeed a most fortunate man."

A well-bred man should never speak to a married woman so pointedly in public. It was permissible to say how well one looked, or it was permissible to merrily compliment the husband on his choice of a lovely wife. But one did not gush over the beauty of another man's wife. Especially in front of her husband.

The duchess was taken aback by the sudden compliment. It was made even more awkward coming from a man who was supposedly courting her sister-in-law. "Thank you, my lord, but it is I who am the most fortunate one." She eyed her husband at the head of the table, and the softness which came over Aldridge's face as he locked gazes with his pretty wife quite shocked Christopher. It was a side of the powerful Duke of Aldridge Christopher had never before seen.

It had been the same with Finch shortly after he'd wed Lady Caroline's sister. An incredible softening had come over him whenever his wife was near, and that overpowering affection strengthened when their son was born. Finch was twice besotted.

"For once I am in perfect agreement with Lord Brockton," Aldridge said with a laugh before he took the decanter to pour more wine into the glasses of the ladies at either side.

"Another thing we have in common, your grace," Brockton said, looking at Lady Caroline, "is our eye for lovely women." The man would not remove his gaze from

Caroline. She looked up at her affianced briefly, and then shyly averted her gaze.

Always the aggressor, she had never averted her gaze from Christopher.

It cut Christopher to the quick to think that never again would he be the recipient of her affections. A hollow, gnawing void was eating into him.

I am the architect of my own misery. And misery it was.

Rothcomb-Smedley began speaking of politics—the only subject upon which that man would ever converse. Even though they were colleagues in the House of Commons, Rothcomb-Smedley to this day remained stiff with Christopher. All because of Caro's scheme to have Christopher pay court to Lady Clair in order to coax Rothcomb-Smedley into declaring his own intentions toward that Ponsby sister. Even though he was now happily married to Lady Clair, Rothcomb-Smedley still believed Christopher hungered after his wife. Could the man not see it had always been Caroline for Christopher?

Political discussion dominated the conversation throughout the remainder of the dinner.

* * *

There had been an awkward moment when the couples were pairing up for whist after dinner. Rothcomb-Smedley put a possessive hand at his wife's waist and positioned himself between her and Mr. Perry, almost shielding her from Perry's line of vision. Good Lord, did the man think Christopher wanted to do the deed with his wife? Caro felt a twinge of guilt for having forced him to feign an attraction to her sister. While Caro's plan had been wildly successfully, Clair's husband would never again be civil to poor Christopher.

Lord Brockton had immediately claimed Caro, and since all the others—save Christopher—were to play with their marital partners, Christopher would have been left out. Fortunately, thought Caro, sweet and selfless Margaret insisted that she preferred to play the pianoforte, thus allowing Christopher to pair with her husband. It was true that Margaret was the most musically inclined in their family, and her play was lovely, but Caro knew how much her sister enjoyed playing whist with her husband.

"Wait!" Morgie said, a self-satisfied look upon his slender face as he peered at Christopher. "You needn't pair up with Finchley. Your Lady Caroline's here! You can play as her partner."

She grimaced. "I am not *his* Lady Caroline. It so happens, Lord Brockton has asked me to be his partner." She turned and took a seat next to his lordship.

"Dear me," said a bewildered Morgie, "I thought . . ."

Lady Lydia quickly linked her arm into her husband's. "Worry not about Mr. Perry, my darling man, I need all your attentions."

Morgie's eyes widened. "Is it your time?"

"No, dearest. It's just that I like you near, and you *are* my favorite whist partner." They sat at the table with the Haverstocks.

Caro was disappointed that she and Lord Brockton would share the table with her brother and his wife. It wouldn't do at all for Aldridge to see that Lord Brockton was an inferior player. She so fiercely wanted to display her intended in a flattering light.

Early into their game, Lord Brockton showed disinterest in his play and interest in the duchess. "What a fortunate man your grace is to have claimed one of the most beautiful women in all of England for your wife. I do envy your domestic felicity." As he spoke, Lord Brockton peered at Elizabeth, rather than at the man he addressed.

This wasn't what Caro had in mind when she told Lord Brockton her brother valued his wife and son more than anything.

Caro found herself peering at Elizabeth, from her pale blond tresses and along the smooth planes of her flawless face. Because she knew her so well, Caro realized his lordship's words had embarrassed the duchess. Even if they were true. Elizabeth was possessed of a fair loveliness that matched her inward beauty and generous spirit. There was an elegance about her countenance that marked her for a duchess long before she and Aldridge came into each other's sphere.

It wasn't her husband's fortune that accounted for the duchess's impeccable taste in fashion. Her eye for lovely clothes was surpassed only by her infinite capacity for charitable works. Caro chuckled to herself. Indeed, it was Elizabeth's charitable works that had inadvertently brought the duke and duchess together.

Instead of being pleased to have his wife's beauty praised, Aldridge glared. "Your play, Brockton."

"My brother takes his play seriously," Caro explained, hoping his lordship would remember to concentrate on the game in order to impress her brother.

Lord Brockton's concentration on the game lasted two more rounds of play before it strayed. "Of course the beauty of the House of Haverstock is matched by the beauty of the Ponsby/Aldridge house." He eyed Caro, and she offered a brittle smile.

"I am proud of all of my sisters," the duke said. "They're as lovely on the inside as on the outside. I daresay I'd kill any man who hurt them in any way." She thought of their eldest sister and the peer who would never return to England and face the wrath of Aldridge. Everyone in the *ton* seemed to know about the man's duplicity.

Her brother once again glared at Lord Brockton, whose play was as unsatisfactory as she had suspected, and they were easily bested by Aldridge and Elizabeth. Twice.

Later that evening, before everyone went to bed, Aldridge complimented Mr. Perry on his ability to beat Mr. Rothcomb-Smedley, who was acknowledged to be an expert whist player. "Thank you, your grace, but I was fortunate to have a good partner." Christopher's gaze went from the duke to Lord Finchley.

"Perry excels at every game—even when we were lads at Eton," Lord Finchley said, eying his lifelong friend with admiration.

Christopher had never easily accepted flattery. "I daresay I merely started playing at an earlier age." He turned to Caro. "How did you fare, my lady?"

He may have spoken flippantly, but the way he studied her with those intense black eyes caused her heartbeat to accelerate. There was something else in his gaze, something she had never before seen. Was it . . . anguish? Was he upset over her betrothal? Did he not know it was his own beastly fault she had pledged to another man? She shrugged. "We lost to the duke and duchess."

Their eyes locked, and neither spoke for a moment. "A sad portent," he finally said. Then he nodded. "I bid you a good night." He turned and left the chamber.

* * *

The following day was Christmas Eve and everyone—including a large assemblage of warmly dressed children—gathered in the entry hall. This was the day the Ponsby family tradition of gathering holly and selecting the Yule log took place. Sulking, Christopher kept his distance from Lady Caroline as she and Brockton stood together. He was as displeased to see her paired with Brockton as he'd been pleased at dinner to see Brockton forced between the dowagers.

Christopher's inner turmoil had prevented him from sleeping the night before, but amidst his torment, one bright revelation had come to him. Even though she had not denied that she was betrothed to Brockton, it was obvious that the couple had not yet announced their intentions to her family. Perhaps there was time to thwart the union.

Gray skies were free of snow, but it was still bitterly cold—a condition that was made even more uncomfortable by a blustery wind. As the large, extended Ponsby-Haverstock families gathered in front of the home's entrance, Christopher flicked a glance at Lady Caroline. She wore a red velvet cloak, its ermine-trimmed hood covering her head. Their eyes briefly met and instantly looked away.

All the women wore hooded cloaks, while

warm woolen mufflers offered the men's ears some protection from the chilling winds.

The children—most of them not much more than babes—were oblivious of the cold. They ran and squealed and frolicked in the novel snow. The oldest, Morgan's lad, showed his cousins how to make snowballs from last night's remaining snow. In no time, they were old hands at hurling the icy spheres at each other as well as at their parents.

As everyone eventually gathered into individual family groups, Christopher once more felt as if he shouldn't have come. He didn't belong here. He watched as Finch lifted his little son as Lady Finchley drew close to her husband and gazed adoringly at little Freddie, who so markedly resembled his dark-haired father. A palpable tenderness stole over the always-amiable Finchley whenever he held his boy. Even his voice gentled.

Christopher's gaze moved to the respected leader of the House of Commons, Rothcomb-Smedley. One of the most powerful men in government was reduced to a babbling idolizer whenever he held his tiny daughter, a cherub with a crown of golden curls.

The very same could be said for the Duke of Aldridge and the Marquess of Haverstock when their toddler sons were present.

Will I ever be like that?

A sleigh was brought around for Lady

Lydia, whose time wasn't that far away. Each of the little ones clamored to join her. Only Lady Finchley would not relinquish her Freddie. "He's too little," she protested. "He might fall out."

"Daresay he'd climb out, the little monkey," his smiling father added.

The sole girl sat on Lady Lydia's lap, the little lads piled in around her. All the others plowed through the thin layer of snow alongside the slow-moving sleigh.

"Don't like Lyddie coming out in this wretched cold," Morgie protested.

Lady Haverstock placed a hand on his sleeve. "You worry too much about her. You always have. She'll be fine."

Morgie stayed as close to the sleigh as he could.

"My darling," Lydia said to him, smiling. "It seems you've put our son's coat on the wrong side out. If you'd allowed him to dress himself—which I assure you he's capable of— he would have done better."

The marchioness giggled. "Your husband does rather smother those he loves, does he not?"

Lydia's long, thin face broke into a smile that made her almost pretty. "I am the most fortunate lady in the kingdom."

Lady Finchley shook her head. "Not true. I am the most fortunate woman in all of England." She smiled adoringly at Finch, whose shimmering gaze met hers as his hand softly stroked her cheek.

Christopher missed his own family more than ever. *I don't belong here.*

When they reached the thicket, Lydia stayed in the sleigh but the children were claimed by their respective parents.

Lord Haverstock went to the Morgans' son, who was the eldest child. "The duke and I are going to need my nephew to help us find the perfect Yule log. Will you oblige us?" The dark-haired lad looked as if he'd grown two inches taller as he nodded, then happily trotted off into the woods with the two men.

Finch came close to Christopher. "Does your family do all this silliness on Christmas Eve?"

Christopher nodded.

"Must be as dull as dirt to an old bachelor like you."

Christopher came even closer and spoke in a low voice. "You've got to help me."

His brows lowered, Finch peered at him. "What's the matter?"

"Lady Caroline's going to marry Brockton."

"The hell you say!"

"So she's not yet told your wife?"

"No, and I can tell you Maggie won't like it above half!" He turned to his wife and motioned for her to join them.

Her eyes not leaving him, Margaret walked across the snow, her progress slowed by their son toddling beside her.

Finch lowered his voice. "Perry says Caro's to marry Brockton."

She shook her head. "I'd know it, if that were true."

Christopher swallowed. "It's true. Lord Brockton told me last night, and your sister confirmed it."

Her face distorted in anguish. "God in heaven, no! That would be disastrous."

"We must stop her," Finch said.

"I shall lock her in the linen closet and tell Lord Brockton she's had a change of heart," Lady Finchley said.

Finch shook his head. "Better if you let Aldridge send Brockton packing—once Lady Caroline's been properly locked in the linen closet."

Christopher shook his head. "No. Lady Caroline must cry off on her own." He eyed Lady Finchley and spoke in a low voice. "Your sister's happiness is very important to me. Brockton can never make her happy."

"Yes," she said with a nod. "John told me what that wretched man said at White's." She shook her head woefully. "Why did she not tell me? I'm the one on earth to whom she's closest."

"For the same reason you didn't tell her when you wed me."

"I knew she would disapprove, and she knows I would disapprove of her choice."

"She must mean to announce it on Christmas Day," Christopher said.

Finch groaned. "Tomorrow."

Lady Finchley winced. "We can't let that happen. We must tell Aldridge."

Finch eyed Christopher. "This would never have happened if you'd just offered for her."

Christopher's eyelids lowered as he drew in a breath and calculated his response. "You know I'm not the marrying kind."

"I know no such thing," Finch spat out. "You've dismissed your ladybird and not replaced her because- -"

Christopher held up a hand. "Pray, don't speak of such in front of a lady."

"I tell my wife everything."

Christopher's gaze went from Finch to his wife. No two people could be better suited, nor more in love. It was as if Lady Finchley truly was her husband's other half. A strange emptiness came over Christopher, like the emptying of a cask. *I want that.*

He drew a deep breath. "We'll not tell Aldridge. Lady Caroline's of age. And she's an obstinate woman. She'll have it her way, with or without her brother's permission."

"Perhaps I can reason with her," Lady Finchley said.

"Then, my lady, I pray that you can," Christopher said with resignation.

"Look," Finch said, his voice guttural, "that scoundrel's trying to lead Caro into the woods. He'll likely steal a kiss—or try to steal much more, knowing his reputation."

Before the sentence was out of Finch's mouth, Christopher had begun to storm across the snow to catch up with the secretly betrothed couple.

$\mathcal{C}$hapter 7

Brockton glared as Christopher neared them, but Christopher acted as if he'd been greeted with open arms. "It seems we're the only ones without children—a common bond, you might say."

"I would say I have little in common with a commoner like you."

Christopher fought the urge to hurl a fist into the man's smug face. To do so would only lower himself to the ill-bred man's level.

Lady Caroline whirled at her betrothed, her pale eyes narrowed to slits. "I daresay Mr. Perry has more friends in the aristocratic class than an earl with the manners of a gutter snipe."

Brockton effected a rueful look but did not apologize.

Nothing would be gained by sinking into Brockton's bilge. Christopher smirked at his opponent. "I do hope you're not attempting to avoid the children. Lady Caroline's exceedingly fond of children—especially her nephews and niece." His gaze flicked to her. "Does your affianced not have nieces and nephews of his own?"

"I . . . I don't know." She peered up at the man to whom she was betrothed, a querying expression on her face.

"I do."

"How many?" she asked.

Brockton shrugged. "Three or four. I don't remember precisely. I find little of interest in children."

Christopher spoke to her as if Brockton were in Coventry—which is precisely where Christopher wished he was. "My, my. You two don't know each other all that well. You didn't know if he had nieces and nephews, and he doesn't know about your love of children. It's not looking as if your intended will ever grace Trent House."

"What the devil is Trent House?" Brockton asked.

"It's not actually Trent House," she answered. "It's a house on Trent Square that --"

"Your brother owns. Everyone knows the Duke of Aldridge owns all of Trent Square," Brockton snapped.

She nodded. "Yes, but this particular house is the duchess's. Even before she married my brother, she selected that house as a refuge for the widows and children of fallen officers. It's her own charity."

"The duchess's—as well as Lady Caroline's and Lady Margaret's and Lady Claire's," Christopher added. "They're all devoted to the women and children there, and each of them helps in her own special way."

She smiled up at him. "Mr. Perry and Lord Finchley have taught them how to play cricket."

"Capital!" Brockton said. "I shall have to make my own contributions at the Trent place,"

"A word of advice," Christopher said. "I wouldn't attempt to try to impart manners. It's not your strong suit, old boy."

Lady Caroline burst out laughing. Humor was something she and Christopher had always shared. A pity she would unite herself to man so vastly different from herself. All they had in common was blue blood.

A little prevarication was called for at present. "You do know," Christopher said to her, "your little Freddie has been calling for his Auntie Caro."

Her eyes lighted. She placed a hand on Brockton's sleeve. "We must go back."

Mission accomplished.

* * *

She was grateful to Mr. Perry for rescuing her from almost certainly having to kiss Lord Brockton. Something was dreadfully wrong with her life if she was going to marry a man she didn't long to kiss. After all, Caro had— ever since she'd cast her affections upon Christopher Perry—craved kissing.

How unhappy that at what should be the

happiest time of her life—the precipice of marriage, something for which she had long sought—she was the most miserable.

As she and Lord Brockton were retracing their steps back to Margaret, Mr. Perry went in the opposite direction, strolling to the sleigh where Mr. Morgan had joined his wife.

She heard her nephew crying before she reached them. It was more of a tantrum crying than an *I'm-hurt* cry. Margaret was having a difficult time keeping her son from putting the red holly berries into his little mouth, and putting them in his mouth was the only thing that held his interest. Lord Finchley, on the other hand, was having a difficult time suppressing his mirth over his son's actions. Margaret and her spouse did so dote on that dear little boy. She fleetingly thought of what kind of father Lord Brockton would make. Not a very good one, she was almost certain.

Another unhappy circumstance. She was beginning to wonder why she had ever thought that marrying him was something to be desired. He had so little to recommend him, other than a handsome countenance and a fine home on Grosvenor Square.

I have made a most deplorable mistake.

Mistake or no mistake, she must go through with it—especially now that she'd told Mr. Perry. She couldn't have him thinking her inconstant.

She groaned inwardly. Constancy of affections had gotten her nowhere.

Kneeling down beside Freddie, she put out her hand. "Give Auntie Caro the pretty holly. I'll hold it for you."

Though his pudgy little fingers had possessively gripped a shredded handful of greenery, he relinquished it to his favorite aunt.

"Pretty," she said.

The remark pleased him so much he set about denuding the holly bush that was nearest and happily handed the little bits of green to her.

"Ah, thank you," she said.

He kept back a red berry and went to pop it into his mouth, but Caro shook her head. "Bad."

He responded by shaking his head.

She withdrew a gloved hand from her muff and held out her palm. After a moment he reluctantly parted with it.

"The little fellow will need longer pieces than those if you're planning to decorate the house for Christmas," Lord Brockton said.

Caro, Margaret and Finchley all glared at Lord Brockton.

"And you'll need to hold your offensive tongue unless you wish to be tossed on the fire with Aldridge's Yule log," the lad's father said.

Since she had known him, Lord Finchley

had never spoken to anyone with such malice. He was the jolliest man imaginable.

Oh, dear, what have I done?

Lord Brockton drew a breath and averted his gaze from the others.

She had pledged herself to a man who was universally hated within her family.

Not understanding the upcoming use for his pointy leaves and snapped-off stems, Freddie offered his next batch to his auntie's male friend. She was relieved when Lord Brockton attempted to act appreciative. "Thank you, young fellow."

She eyed him. "His name is Freddie."

"And a very nice name it is." He looked up at Lord Finchley like an errant child seeking approval.

But Lord Finchley's congeniality was like a woman' virginity—once forfeited, never regained.

Freddie's concentration on the task at hand was soon distracted by the duke's dog. No matter that it was twice his size, Freddie began to run after it. As did his other cousins. Soon all the children were running around in circles, squealing.

Caro wished she could. Perhaps then she wouldn't be so beastly cold.

The frolicking came to an end when Aldridge and Lord Haverstock emerged from the wood with a thick, short log. "See what a fine job Simon has done in selecting the perfect log," Aldridge said.

Simon Morgan straightened his three and a half feet as if he were as tall as his uncles, a smile lifting his face.

Caro's gaze shifted to the sleigh to see that Simon's parents had seen their son praised, but neither seemed to be aware their son had reappeared.

Then Mr. Perry, a look of concern etched into his face, came rushing up to Lord Haverstock. "I believe your sister's time has come."

"Oh, dear," exclaimed the duchess, who was nearby. She then rushed off to see to her sister. "This is far too early."

* * *

While the women attended Lady Lydia, all the men gathered in the library. Such a gathering in one of the most intimate rooms in the house should have been comforting, but it was not. A gloom hung in the chilly air like a menacing fog.

It was obvious to Christopher that Aldridge was being uncommonly jolly in order to lessen Morgie's uncommonly grim demeanor. What a good friend Aldridge was. Christopher could almost imagine him as the lad he'd been when he befriended Haverstock and Morgie at Eton. The duke who rarely allowed anyone to observe his softer side was now acting almost the buffoon.

"You could name this next son Half Baked,

or there's always Organ. I like the sound, Organ Morgan. What say you, Haverstock? Should you like a nephew named Organ Morgan?" Aldridge, who sat on a sofa in the darkly paneled library, looked from Morgie at his left to Haverstock on his right.

Haverstock, who was trying to hide his fears for his sister, shook his head. "Lydia's much too sensible to allow that. She would likely know what object men might refer to as an organ."

"My Lyddie's very musical," Morgie said.

"Not that organ," Haverstock quipped.

Morgie drew a deep breath and leapt to his feet, coming to stand before the fire. "When will that accoucheur arrive?"

"Even if he's not in time," Aldridge said, "Lady Lydia's surrounded by experienced women—including her mother. You can be assured she's in good hands."

"Yes," Haverstock said. "Mother not only was brought to bed nine times herself—three of our siblings were lost in infancy—but she's been with each of my sisters when their time came—and she did a masterful job when my son was born."

"He came early, too, did he not?" Finch said, smiling at Lord Haverstock.

Haverstock shook his head. "Quite to opposite. Our son was very late. Nothing about my wife's pregnancy was easy or common, but I'm quite sure that made for one perfect child." He cracked a smile. "Your child will be perfect, too, Morgie."

"It's not the child I'm worried about," Morgie snapped.

Christopher tried to imagine how he would feel if Lady Caroline was the one lying in pain in the room above. Even if she were married to another, he realized he would never stop caring for her, never stop hurting when she hurt.

None of these reassuring comments was capable of lifting the gloom from this chamber. Perhaps it was the dreariness of the weather. Even this, the warmest room of the house, was as cold as a tomb. Christopher got to his feet. "Who's up for a game of billiards?"

Aldridge stood. "A capital idea."

Morgie shook his head. "I can't. Not when Lyddie's in danger."

"Your wife is not in danger," Aldridge said sternly.

"I feel it in my bones."

Now Haverstock stood. "You've always worried too much about her, and you've never been right in your fears. Lydia's as strong as an ox. I daresay she'll outlive every one of us."

The aged oak door squeaked open, and there stood the Aldridge's stooped-over butler. Never a friendly sort, the old fellow looked even more somber than normal. His gaze went to Morgie, and he cleared his throat.

"Mr. Morgan may come now to see his wife. She's . . . " He paused, his thick white brows lowering. "She's passed away."

$\mathcal{C}$hapter 8

Amidst the cries of anguish, Christopher kept a cool head. Too many times he'd experienced the butler's mangling of words. He raced up the stairs on Morgie's heels. "Perhaps Barrow has miscommunicated."

Aldridge stopped almost in mid stride, a firm hand on his old friend. "He may be right, Morgie. Surely Barrow's mistaken, owing to his hearing impairment."

Morgie did not stop but continued hurrying to see his wife's body.

It wasn't Christopher's place to be there, but he was strangely compelled to join the press of anxious men. Only Brockton stayed below.

When they reached the landing, Lady Caroline was emerging from Lady Lydia's chamber, a smile on her face.

What the devil?

When she saw the stricken look on Morgie's face, she said, "Pray, Mr. Morgan, do not let Lady Lydia see you like this. You mustn't show her you're disappointed to have a daughter."

Tears rushed down Morgie's face. "Lydia's

not dead?"

Lady Caroline's eyes widened. "I told Barrow to tell you she was at last awake."

Christopher stepped forward. "Apparently Barrow took *last awake* for *passed away*, poor chap."

Morgie had not heard. He flew into the chamber where his wife and daughter lay in the darkness.

The dowager Haverstock and the other women left the two alone.

"Then all is well with Lady Lydia?" Christopher asked Lady Caroline.

"At last!"

They both laughed.

"I pray she didn't suffer too greatly."

"Her suffering has been well compensated."

The babe. Lady Caroline was as child-mad as her sister, Lady Finchley. It was a shame she was willing to wed the blackguard Brockton in order to become a mother.

His hand touched hers. "The child who has you for a mother will be blessed indeed." He turned and left.

* * *

The anxiety of those long hours of Lady Lydia's lying in had put such a strain on the gathering that the large Christmas Eve dinner had been postponed until Christmas Day. They all went early to their beds. In spite of her physical exhaustion and the recurrent memory of Lady Lydia's difficult birth, Caro was unable to sleep.

She kept remembering Christopher's words when he'd referred to her having a child. Only a man in love could have spoken with such tenderness. Why had life so cruelly robbed her of marrying the man she loved? Why was Christopher so averse to marrying?

She thought of how dislikable Lord Brockton was. She thought of how unsatisfactory his kisses were. She came to realize that even if it meant she could never have a home of her own, never become a mother, she could not marry him.

It was a monumental decision. Thank God she'd never told her family about her betrothal. That would have made it so much more difficult to break the engagement.

When could she do so? A pity they'd all gone to bed so early. She must cry off before the family gathered tomorrow afternoon for Christmas dinner. She began to rehearse the words she would use.

Even with that decision made, she still could not sleep. Not when Christopher Perry lay sleeping just down the corridor from her. She loved him still with every beat of her heart and always would. Would she die an old maid all for the love of him?

* * *

Sleep eluded Christopher. He'd never given much thought to love—real love like that of Morgie for his cherished wife. After the satisfactory completion of Lady Lydia's lying in, Finch had explained how upset he'd been. "I knew just exactly how Morgie felt," Finch had said, "for I kept thinking of how I'd feel if it had been my Maggie."

Did every man here at Glenmont love that deeply? He thought back to his own parents and remembered how devoted they were to each other, remembered his mother's devastation when Papa died. She was still young and beautiful and sought after, but vowed that she would never love again.

Will I ever love like that? The answer was ridiculously simple. He would always love like that. That's why he'd dismissed his mistress. There was only one woman he'd ever love, and that woman was Lady Caroline Ponsby.

As he lay there peering into the flickering fire, he heard a door opening. He was almost certain it was Brockton's door for he was in the next room. Was that defiler of women going to try to sneak into Lady Caroline's bedchamber?

Christopher leapt from his bed. Betrothed or not, Christopher would not stand for it! He quickly stepped into his breeches and eased open his door to peer down the corridor, which was lighted by wall sconces at fifteen-foot intervals. Surprisingly, a fully-dressed Brockton strode right past Lady Caroline's room.

Why in the devil was the man carrying a

candle? Aldridge saw to it that every corridor was well lighted throughout the night.

As long as Brockton was not forcing himself on Lady Caroline, his actions were of no interest to Christopher. He quietly closed the door.

Returned to his bed, he went to close the velvet drapes around it but decided against it. As long as the fire burned, the bedchamber was tolerable. Perhaps later, when the fire died out, he would close the drapes for warmth.

He propped himself on pillows, watching the sputtering fire grow weaker and weaker until it softly died. When Brockton did not return to his room, Christopher decided to investigate. After all, the man had a nasty reputation. Perhaps he was nicking the ducal silver.

Fully dressed, Christopher left his room— and immediately smelled smoke. Not from this floor—from higher up. *Good Lord!* Could it be from the nursery? His heart pounding, Christopher raced down the corridor and flew up the wooden staircase to the top floor. Beneath the glow of a wall sconce stood Brockton. There was no candle in his hand. *Dear God!*

He knew he must act quickly. He knew, too, that he couldn't do this alone. He yelled as if he were on the top of a mountain trying to be heard far below. "Fire! Fire!"

Christopher must find the children! He stormed past Brockton, cursing as he elbowed him as hard as he could. The wooden door was ablaze. Christopher froze for a moment. This close to the blaze, the heat was so intense he felt as if he could melt into a pile of ash. *I have to run through fire to save the children.*

He could die. But, unlike Brockton, he couldn't live with himself if he didn't try.

He took a deep breath, said a prayer, and charged through the blazing doorway. His body became an inferno. The wall of fire, thankfully, had not migrated into the chamber. Once he was past it, he threw himself to the carpet and rolled, then leapt to his feet and peeled off his charred jacket and used it to cover his singed hair for a moment.

Oddly, he wasn't aware of his pain. All that mattered was the children.

His initial cries must have awakened the lad who slept here as well as his nurse who emerged from a little alcove. She leapt into the boy's smoky chamber, screaming hysterically.

Through the smoke, Christopher recognized the lad as little Ram, the duke's lad and a most cherished nephew of Lady Caroline. The little fellow sat up in his bed, coughing and regarding Christopher with huge, frightened eyes.

Christopher scooped him into his arms.

They couldn't go out through the wall of fire. They'd have to go out this third-floor window.

"Come with us," he shouted to the crying nurse.

She nodded, then raced to the window as smoke swelled through the room. The fire chased them. She threw open the casements, and with a wail and one crazed look back at her charge, she hoisted herself upon the window. And she leapt into the darkness.

Her fading cries would haunt him until the day he died.

Which might be today.

Blast it all! There was no ledge. Holding tightly to the lad while straddling the windowsill, he cried out again with the same force he'd used earlier. "Help! Help!"

Someone must toss them a rope or bring a ladder. Something. Jumping down three stories might be quicker than burning to death but just as fatal.

He was curious to see if the nurse had survived her fall, but the night was too black.

He must try to scale the stone wall like a deformed spider.

"Ram," he said to the shivering, whimpering lad, "you're to hold on to me as tightly as you can and do not let go. I will need my hands to climb down this wall. Do you understand?"

"Yes."

"Good. I shall need you to ride piggy-back

style from behind. Do you understand?"

"Yes."

Christopher turned so that the boy could mount his back.

The lad clung to him as he positioned himself on Christopher's shoulders.

Christopher lowered himself from the window, his hands clutching the windowsill until he could get a foothold between the stones.

His hands were getting hotter as the raging fire ate up the lad's room and threatened to follow them out the window. If he could descend further, he would have, but there was nothing he could stand upon. He would have to keep holding on until the flames lapped at his fingers.

Amidst his prayers for help, voices from below broke through the horror like a bolt of light on the darkest night.

"We've got a ladder!" The duke said. "Are you all right, Ram?" His voice was anguished.

"Yes, Papa!"

Please hurry. The heat shot through his painful fingers. He hoped to God he could hold on long enough to get the boy to safety.

The top of the ladder banged twice against the wall before it came to settle within five feet of Christopher's boots. The duke was climbing upwards, his face lighted by the fire that had almost reached Christopher's fingers. When he came as high as he could climb, he said, "Son, you must carefully climb down Mr. Perry's body until your Papa can reach you."

Christopher did not know how much longer he would be able to hold on. If it weren't for the child, he would have plunged into the darkness as the nurse had done. It was as if his hands had been tied to a boiling cauldron. He grimaced in unbearable pain. Tears shot from his eyes.

The lad shimmied down Christopher's back. Then his legs. When his little hands closed around Christopher's ankles, the duke was able to snatch his dangling son to carry him to safety.

But the duke merely handed the boy off to the next person on the ladder. "Don't drop, Perry. We'll get you."

Christopher couldn't hold on. The fire was too close. He drew a deep breath in preparation of dropping to almost certain death.

"Quick, Perry!" Aldridge said. "We've got another ladder. It's taller. Just to your right."

The thudding sound of that second ladder solidly anchoring against the wall was the best sound he'd ever heard.

As he hung on with only his left hand, Christopher's dangling right leg found the top rung of the second ladder, and he planted one boot on it. Thank God this ladder was tall enough! Then he let go the other hand and hoped his left foot would steady on the ladder. He had to brace himself against the wall by flattening his hands against it. The pain seared from his fingers though his arms. But he remained upright.

* * *

Tears streamed down Caro's face when Elizabeth's arms closed around her crying son. *Thank God little Ram had made it!*

Horror gripped her as she looked upward to see the rectangle of flame leaping from the window of what had been Ram's bedchamber, a blaze of light from the fire illuminating Christopher's sleek bare back. His hand disengaged from that same window and his dangling foot searched for a solid foothold. It was as if the ability to breathe had been sucked from her body. She couldn't watch.

A scream broke from her, and tears gushed as her head twisted away.

The cacophony of frantic voices hushed. The chilly, black night went silent. It was as if the dozen people who surrounded her all held their breath.

Her eyes shuttered, she prayed.

Then as quickly as the crowd had hushed, a roar of cheers went up.

Christopher's safe!

She could breathe again.

Tears streamed down her happy face as she watched him descend the ladder that was anchored at the bottom by a half dozen strong footmen and her brother.

Aldridge was the first to greet him, attempting to shake his hand.

But Christopher withdrew it, wincing.

His hands had been burned.

She rushed to him and threw herself into his arms. As his arms slowly closed around her, she thought this was the happiest moment in her life. "You're hurt, my darling," she murmured.

"I've never been better," he said throatily.

"I thank you from the bottom of my heart," a choked-up Aldridge said. "I would be honored to have you as a member of our family."

She gazed up at the man she loved. "And I, dear man, would have perished if something had happened to you."

His brows lowered. "What about that damned Brockton?"

She shook her head. "I could never have married him. Not when I love you, you goose."

Christopher eyed the duke, who wore an amused expression. "What about the nurse?" He knew how impossible it would have been to survive a fall from three stories, but he hoped he was wrong.

The duke sadly shook his head.

Fury bolted through Christopher. "Then Brockton's a bloody murderer. He started the fire."

Aldridge looked as angry as the blaze. "You

mean this was deliberately set? Why would anyone want to kill my son?"

She gasped and turned to her brother. "Lord Brockton wanted to be a hero to impress you."

"So that explains it," Christopher said. "He didn't have the guts to run through flames to save the lad."

That explained why Christopher was shirtless. "You went through flames to save my nephew?"

Before he could answer, Aldridge uttered, "My God, Perry. You're the bravest man in England. I owe you everything I possess."

"You owe me nothing." Christopher gazed tenderly at Caro. "But I would be honored to win the hand of your sister."

He'd said it! He'd finally said the words she'd been longing to hear every day for almost two years.

"Nothing could make me happier," Aldridge said. He turned away. "Except perhaps killing Brockton." He strode off angrily.

She knew her brother was too controlled to actually kill her former fiancé, but when Aldridge was finished with Lord Brockton, the earl might wish he were dead. One thing was sure. Lord Brockton would never again be seen in England. He wouldn't be the first man Aldridge had banished from his homeland.

A coatless Lord Haverstock met them at the door and told them the fire had been put out, and all the children were safe.

She sighed. "Thank God. Now, my soon-to-be husband and owner of my heart, we must see to your hands."

Chapter 9

They all sat at the long table for Christmas dinner. Every child was permitted to attend on this special day—even if their messes were enough to dampen appetites.

Caro sat next to Christopher, whose hands were bandaged and, for now, unless. She fed him as if he were her own much-loved child.

After the goose was picked clean and the sweetmeats laid, Aldridge, who sat at the head of the table, tapped his claret glass with a spoon to get everyone's attention. When every eye went to him, he looked affectionately at his son, then cast a solemn look at Christopher. "I think it's appropriate on this day to give thanks. I am blessed to have a wife and son whom I cherish, and I'm particularly grateful to Mr. Perry for risking his life to save my beloved son." He smiled, drew a breath, and continued. "It is with profound joy that I announce the betrothal of Mr. Perry and my sister Caroline. I've been waiting for a very long to make this welcome announcement. You two are perfect for one another."

"I've always thought so," Caro said, looking

up at her Christopher with worshipping eyes.

Christopher smiled at Aldridge. "Thank you, your grace. I must own that I have been a bit intimidated by you and am, therefore, grateful to learn that you approved of me— even before last night."

"If you hadn't offered for her by today, I was ready to prod you with a musket."

Caro was relieved that her brother approved of Christopher. "I must apologize for inviting that wretched man here." She was embarrassed and ashamed. "I had lost hope of marrying the man I've loved for so long . . ."

Morgie piped up. "Ah, so that's why that bugger was here! You were trying to make old Perry jealous."

"Not exactly," she said. "I had lost all hope and was trying to fall in love with that odious man." She looked back at Christopher. "I had planned—even before the fire—to send him away today. I knew I could not go through with marrying him"

They all expressed their mutual contempt.

"While we're making confessions," Lord Haverstock said, turning to his wife, "I have one to make. Forgive me if I've been distant as of late. I'd taken a huge risk that I feared was going to clean us out. It occupied all my thoughts, but I'm happy to say that all's well. I'd mortgaged the castle in Ireland for a risky investment that finally came back up two days ago. I sold all the stock for a good profit, bought back the castle and am well-fixed now."

Lady Haverstock laughed. "I knew you'd been worried about finances so I sold my mother's necklace. I planned to give you the money today. For Christmas."

"That priceless thing from your father?" Lord Haverstock asked.

The marchioness nodded.

He took her hands in his. "I'm buying it back, my dearest. It's all you've got left from your father. I had hoped perhaps - -"

Caro knew he had meant to say that he hoped the necklace would one day go to a daughter of theirs, but he'd stopped out of sensitivity to his wife's fears that she would never again conceive. Everyone—including the Haverstocks themselves—had almost lost hope that she would ever bear the Haverstock heir. It had taken two pregnancies and almost four years.

Anna Haverstock smiled. It wasn't an everyday smile but one that could cast a beacon on a dark night. "I have an announcement to all our family and those we love most." Her happy gaze went around the table and came to settle on her doting husband. "We shall once again be blessed with another child—God willing to see me through these next seven months."

Caro watched the marquess swallow back his emotions. She wasn't sure from where she sat some distance away, but Caro thought there was a tear in his eye.

"And I have an announcement to make," Morgie said. The joyful expression on his face was the exact opposite of what it had been the night before when Caro had faced him just outside Lady Lydia's lying-in room. "Lyddie has agreed to allow me to name our beautiful baby girl. She shall be called Lydia—after her beautiful mother."

No one at that table would have considered Lady Lydia a beauty—no one except someone deeply in love.

Every face shone with happy smiles. The dowager Lady Haverstock said, "A good choice. I've always loved the name Lydia. That's why I gave it to my firstborn, my beautiful baby daughter."

Everyone's smiles went even deeper, and happiness filled the chamber like an uplifting cloud.

"John and I have an announcement to make," Margaret said shyly.

Margaret must be increasing! And she'd not told Caro? It had always stung that Lord Finchley had supplanted her in her sister's affections. They were still the closest of sisters, but Lord Finchley was always first in Margaret's heart.

Will Christopher and I be like them? She did so hope that they would.

Margaret and Lord Finchley exchanged

adoring gazes and then Lord Finchley nodded. "Yes, my wife is once again with child. I hope it will be a little girl as beautiful as she is."

Now Caro had a tear in her eye. She was so happy the sister she loved so dearly had for a husband a man who adored Margaret as she deserved. Caro's gaze went from the happy couple down the table to the dowager Finchley, whose happiness could not be suppressed. "It's about time we have a little girl in the Finchley family! Whatever it is, I shall be most thankful for another great-grandchild."

* * *

Christopher didn't care how bloody cold it was. He was going to take a sleigh ride through the snow with his Caroline before the sun set. His eyes shimmered as she came to him, wrapped in her red velvet cloak, the pure ermine haloing her lovely face. Her hands were stuffed in an ermine muff.

She moved silently to him and slipped her arm into his, and they left the house. She insisted on holding the reins to spare his injured hands, and they slowly plowed through the snow. No words were necessary. They were together. They loved each other. That was enough. They came to the same thicket where Aldridge had found the Yule log. They stopped and he drew her into his arms.

Though every time he'd ever kissed Caroline had been magical, this was the most potent kiss ever. They both felt it. He wasn't sure where he left off and where she began. It was as if they had blended into one warm, passionate being.

He held her for a long time afterward, and then he said quite simply. "I'll get a special license tomorrow. I don't give a fig about contracts. You're going to be my wife in two days."

She nodded. "I'd marry you today, if we could. It's all I've wanted since the day we met."

He nodded. He'd always known that what she felt for him was more profound than what she would ever feel for another man, but somehow he'd never thought Society would approve of their match. After all, she *was* the daughter of a duke. But that no longer mattered. It mattered not to her. Not to Aldridge. Apparently not to anyone but him. "I've been a fool," he finally said. "I should have married you the moment I knew I loved you."

"And when was that?"

"I think I loved you from that first day. I didn't know it until . . ."

"Until you couldn't make love to your mistress anymore?"

His eyes widened. "How did you know?"

"I didn't. Unbelievably, it was Lord Finchley

who worked that one out. He told Margaret you must be in love with me because a man truly in love with one woman could not make love with another. At least that's how an honorable man like Lord Finchley thinks."

Christopher nodded. Finch was an honorable man. "I didn't want you to know about that business. It's you and only you I've ever loved."

She kissed his bandaged hands. "I know."

"And how does a maiden know about things like a man desiring a woman?"

She spoke huskily. "This maiden is most passionate. But only for you, my darling. Always and ever, it's been you."

His lips settled softly upon hers. "I promise you, my love, next Christmas you'll have our child. I know how much you long to be a mother."

She slipped her gloved hand from her muff and gently stoked his face. "I do, but even if I prove to be barren, I'll never be unhappy as long as I have your love."

The End

Dear Reader,

Thank you for reading *Ex-Spinster by Christmas*. If you would like to keep up with my new releases and other writing news, you can subscribe to my occasional newsletter at www.cherylbolen.com.

House of Haverstock Series

If you have not read the other books in the House of Haverstock series, you might enjoy reading the first three installments which were full-length novels.

Lady by Chance (Book 1)

The Marquess of Haverstock is incensed when he learns the money he needed to buy crucial war information for the Foreign Office has been lost at cards to the illegitimate daughter of an English duke and French noblewoman. When the bewitchingly beautiful woman informs him the only way to reclaim the funds is to wed her, he has little choice but to agree.

Shunned by the ton, Anna de Mouchet agrees to a bizarre proposal that has her using her skill at cards to force the marquess – whom she's been told is a traitor – to marry her. As his wife, she will be free to spy on him and prove her patriotism to England. But once she marries the handsome lord, she's less sure of her loyalties. Especially when she feels her husband's silken touch.

Duchess by Mistake (Book 2)

An innocent visit to the Duke of Aldridge's to request a donation for her war widows puts Lady Elizabeth Upton in the midst of a most shocking scandal. . .

The Duke of Aldridge offers for his best friend's sister, Lady Elizabeth Upton, after a mix-up sends her to his bedchamber—just as he's emerging from his bath. She most certainly does not want to force the duke's hand, but how can she bear the shame her scandalous behavior has cast upon her dear brother, the Marquess of Haverstock?

Once she agrees to marry her childhood heartthrob, Elizabeth realizes she wants nothing more than to win her husband's love. But capturing his heart is no easy task when former loves threaten to destroy the fragile bonds of their marriage.

Countess by Coincidence (Book 3)

Two staggering coincidences result in the marriage of the reckless young Earl of Finchley and Lady Margaret Ponsby, a shy duke's daughter who's worshipped him from afar. . .

To extricate himself from financial difficulties, John Beauclerc, the Earl of Finchley, concocts a scheme to marry a stranger who's answered his advertisement. He'll show his grandmother! That lady's withholding money until he can demonstrate more maturity and less scandalous behavior. At six and twenty, the last thing he wants is to settle down. He goes to the church at St. George's Hanover Square to wed Miss Margaret Ponsby of Windsor, send her on her way with £100, and continue to pursue wine, women and faro with his fun-seeking friends.

After the ceremony, he realizes he's married the wrong woman. Miss Margaret Ponsby of Windsor obviously thought the wedding was to occur at St. George's Chapel in Windsor. Lady Margaret Ponsby was at St. George's in London. How can he extricate himself from this wretched marriage—a marriage over which his grandmother is ecstatic?

Author's Biography

A former journalist and English teacher, Cheryl Bolen sold her first book to Harlequin Historical in 1997. That book, *A Duke Deceived*, was a finalist for the Holt Medallion for Best First Book, and it netted her the title Notable New Author. Since then she has published more than 20 books with Kensington/Zebra, Love Inspired Historical and was Montlake launch author for Kindle Serials. As an independent author, she has broken into the top 5 on the *New York Times* and top 20 on the *USA Today* best-seller lists.

Her 2005 book *One Golden Ring* won the Holt Medallion for Best Historical, and her 2011 gothic historical *My Lord Wicked* was awarded Best Historical in the International Digital Awards, the same year one of her Christmas novellas was chosen as Best Historical Novella by Hearts Through History. Her books have been finalists for other awards, including the Daphne du Maurier, and have been translated into eight languages.

She invites readers to www.CherylBolen.com, or her blog, www.cherylsregencyramblings.wordpress.co or Facebook at https://www.facebook.com/pages/Cheryl-Bolen-Books/146842652076424.

58133283R00076

Made in the USA
Lexington, KY
04 December 2016